BIRMINGHAM
THEATRES
CONCERT & MUSIC HALLS

By the same author

By the same author

BIRMINGHAM CINEMAS

OLD LADYWOOD REMEMBERED

BIRMINGHAM
THEATRES
CONCERT & MUSIC HALLS

1740 – 1988

Victor J. Price

Foreword by Derek Salberg

BREWIN BOOKS

First published in April 1988 by
K.A.F. Brewin Books, Studley,
Warwickshire. B80 7LX

From — "As You Like It"

All the world's a stage,
And all the men and women merely players:
They have their exits and their entrances;
And one man in his life plays many parts,
His acts being seven ages.

W. Shakespeare.

ISBN 0 947731 35 0

Typeset in Baskerville 11pt.
and made and printed in Great Britain by
Supaprint (Redditch) Ltd., Redditch, Worcs.

FOREWORD

I was highly complimented that Victor J. Price should have asked me to write the Foreword to this book, especially as I had thoroughly enjoyed his first book, 'Birmingham Cinemas 1900–1960' and was looking forward to reading this, his most recent book, and I was certainly not disappointed. It not only abounds in a profusion of fascinating photographs of theatres and theatrical performers but also equally fascinating playbills, programmes and advertisements. The book also documents every theatre and hall (and it is a long list) which have existed in Birmingham, since the first, the Moor Street Theatre in 1740, some for a brief span, others to achieve great success and some national and even international fame.

Deservedly, too, as the amateur movement is particularly strong in the area, the author has included many of the amateur theatres and companies.

Space is also found for many of Birmingham's other buildings, not entirely confined to entertainment. These include the Town Hall, Bingley Hall (at one time a permanent theatre) the Birmingham and Midland Institute, Curzon Hall, Kings Hall, the Temperance and Masonic Halls and many more. He also pays tribute to the contributions made by such groups as the Arden Singers and the Betty Fox Babes (who have appeared in virtually every major city in England).

These are only a few of the items the author has included in this splendidly researched and fascinating book, which visibly recalls so much of the glitter and glamour and occasionally depressing story of Birmingham's long theatrical history.

In brief it is a book which will delight everyone who has a love of things theatrical and indeed of Birmingham itself.

Victor J. Price clearly has both, which shine throughout its pages.

Derek S. Salberg.

INDEX

PREFACE

The Live theatre has, for over two centuries, been an attraction to the citizens of Birmingham and the aspiration of many to act or to receive training in the art. Many well known actors and actresses received their baptism in the art in this City.

In the beginning this type of entertainment was in the form of roaming players, who gave performances and travelled from town to town.

This is a potted history of the theatres, concert and music halls in Birmingham. The first theatre to be opened was the 'New Theatre' in Moor Street in 1740.

Long before the days of radio and T.V. when people had to make their own amusement, Birmingham, like many other towns, had numerous music halls. These were, in effect, the working man's theatre. They started in the Inns and Beer Houses, as they were then called, giving entertainment to customers. The proprietors opened special rooms adjacent to the premises for this purpose and they became extremely popular. A list of the popular music hall songs can be found on page 60. Monologues also became popular together with juggling and magic acts.

In the early 1800's there was considerable controversy on the question of whether to allow the erection of further theatres or not, there being a strong non-conformist opinion that was opposed to such projects on the grounds that it was thought immoral. Matthew Boulton, the industrialist and a literal minded gentleman was strongly in favour of such an enterprise. The debt owed to his spirited efforts is too little known, in consequence of his efforts permission was granted by the Government to continue with the project. He was later appointed one of the directors of the Theatre Royal.

I have also included the Amateur Theatres in Birmingham for they, too, have contributed to the enjoyment of the citizens of this City by the presentation of popular plays and pantomimes over the years.

Photographs of 50 of the actors and actresses are included from the early 1900's to the present day. The majority of these have performed at the Theatres in this city.

In the back of the book are listed Actors, Actresses and Theatrical celebrities born in Birmingham and area.

My first experience of live theatre was when I was attending St. John's School in Ladywood in the early 1930's. The teachers erected a stage, with props and curtains, and put on a play, 'The Monkey's Paw' by Louis N. Parker. I was enthralled, as I had never experienced anything like this before. All the parts were played by the teaching staff.

My next experience was at the Prince of Wales Theatre in Broad Street, when I was 12 years of age, I was selected, with 11 other choristers from St. Martin's Church in the Bull Ring, to play and sing in two operas, Carmen and Tosca in June 1932. A week of operas was presented and the proceeds in aid of the General, Queen's and Ear and Throat Hospitals.

In the mid 1930's I went again, to the Prince of Wales Theatre to see my first professional performance, 'Charley's Aunt'. The part of Charley was played by Arthur Askey. This was the beginning of my theatrical experiences. I attended numerous pantomimes at the Alexandra Theatre and the Birmingham Hippodrome. I was never an ardent patron but I do have happy memories of those early days in my life.

Victor J. Price.

CONTENTS

MOOR ST. THEATRE

By a Company of Comedians from London
The present evening being the 29th of this
instant will be revived
THE TEMPEST
(or The Enchanted Island)
as altered by Mr. Dryden and
Sir William Davenant concluding with a
Grand Masque of
NEPTUNE and AMPHITRITE
No person can be admitted back stage on account
of the machinery
Boxes and Stage: 2/6   Pit 2/-   Balconies 2/-
To begin punctually at 7 o'clock
VIVAT REX

Positively the last Time of Mrs. MATTOCKSs performing
By Their MAJESTIES Servants.
At the Theatre in King-Street,
This present WEDNESDAY, September 20, 1775.
Will be presented (not Acted here this Season) the COMEDY of

AS YOU LIKE IT.

(Written by SHAKESPEAR)
Orlando by Mr. WARD.
Jaques Mr. JACKSON.
Touchstone Mr. T. KENNEDY.
Oliver Mr. CUMMINS.
Duke Senior Mr. KENNEDY.
Amiens (with Songs) Mr. BARNSHAW.
Duke Frederick Mr. GLOSTER.
Le Beu Mr. BATES.
William Mr. HOLLINGSWORTH.
(Being his First Appearance on this Stage)
Silvius Mr. SMITH.
Jaques de Bois Mr. TAYLOR.
AND
Adam Mr. YOUNGER.
Phebe Miss ATKINSON.
Celia Miss FARRELL.
Audrey Miss K. FARREN.
And Rosalind (with the Song of the Cuckoo)
By Mrs. MATTOCKS.
End of Act First, a Dance called *The Old Ground Young*, by Master
LANGRIDGE and Miss LINGS.
End of the PLAY a Dance by Master LANGRIDGE
and Miss LINGS.
To which will be added

The CITIZEN.

Young Philpot Mr. T. KENNEDY.
Old Philpot Mr. HOLLINGSWORTH.
Sir Jasper Wilding (with a Song in Character) Mr. BARNSHAW.
Young Wilding Mr. TAYLOR.   Beaufort Mr. SMITH.
Dapper Mr. GLOSTER   Quildrive Mr. BATES.
Corinna Miss ATKINSON.
AND THE PART OF
Maria by Mrs. MATTOCKS.
In which Character She will accompany herself in a *French Song* on the
Guitar and Dance a *Minuet* with Mr. LANGRIDGE.

On Friday, The ROYAL CONVERT, for the Benefit of
Mr. TAYLOR, Miss FARRELL and Miss SINGLETON.

MOOR STREET THEATRE, Moor Street. Opened in 1740 and is the earliest record of a theatre in Birmingham. It was not a purpose built theatre. The opening performance being an Oratorio with Vocal and Instrumental Musick. In August 1744 The Tempest was presented, (see small advertisement for full details). On another occasion an Evening of Entertainment was arranged, 'For the benefit of Dr. Heighington and Mr. Gunn'. Several musical compositions were performed. Owing to the cold weather at the time, the theatre was warmed by fires kept burning for two days before the performance. After the concert a Ball was held for members of the public purchasing pit tickets. Although attendance at the theatre was, when it opened, satisfactory, it eventually closed in 1764 and the building was taken over by the Methodists and converted into a Chapel. John Westley, one of the founders of the Methodists, preached there at the opening service.

THE THEATRE, in King Street. This was the first purpose built theatre in the city, built by Richard Yates and opened on the 25th September 1751, the first performance being a Shakespeare Night and Concert of Vocal and Instrumental Musicians. It held numerous concerts and performances for the benefit of the General Hospital. There was no National Health Service in those days and the hospital relied on donations and subscriptions to survive. Prices of admission 3s, 2s and 1s. It was enlarged in 1774 and had elegant fittings, chandeliers and decoration. It closed c 1779 and the building was sold to the Countess of Huntingdon, founder of Calvinistic religious association called the Countess of Huntingdon's Conexion. The area was demolished later when New Street Station and the Queen's Hotel was erected.

THEATRE ROYAL, New Street.

This was the second theatre to be built in Birmingham. It opened on the 20th June 1774. It was then called "The New Theatre". The manager was Richard Yates. It had a handsome sandstone facade which withstood two disastrous fires, one in 1792 and the other in 1820. It was described by Hutton, the local historian as "One of the finest theatres in the world". It had a seating capacity of 2000. In the upper compartment were displayed two medallions, of excellent workmanship, in relief, of Shakespeare and Garrick. These are now erected on display in the Birmingham Central Library.

The first performance was advertised as a Concert of Music. Prices of admission, Boxes 3/-, Pit 2/-, Gallery 1/-. Between the several parts of the concert, a Company of Their Majesties Comedians from the Theatre Royal in London, gave performances (gratis) of the Shakespeare comedy, "As you like It".

After the 1792 fire it was restored and re-opened on Monday 23rd June 1794 under the management of Mr. W. McCready, author of the comedy "Bank Note". The seats were covered in crimson and the cushions in apple green. It had two tiers and 16 boxes.

After the second fire, which occurred on 6th January 1820 just after the performance of the play "Pizarro", the whole interior and roof were reduced to ashes in a very short time. It was re-opened on the 14th August in the same year after being re-built and Gas Lighting installed, showing Sheridan's Comedy, "The Rivals" to which was added a new farce, "The Promissory Note". The orchestra was conducted by Mr. Parnell. The theatre was ornamented by 20 brilliant chandeliers.

Over the years numerous musical festivals were organised and the proceeds donated to charities. In 1791, for example, Dorothy Jordon, a famous actress of the day, gave a performance of "The Country Girl" by Garrick. She played the part of Peggy. A donation of £62.13.1 was presented to the General Hospital from the proceeds of this production. Miss Jordan later became the mistress of King William IV.

In 1802 Lord Nelson, accompanied by Sir William and Lady Hamilton, attended, to see the production of "The Merry Wives of Windsor". This was the first of many visits to the theatre by Lord Nelson. It was granted the Royal Title in 1807.

On the 4th January 1902, with the showing of the comedy, "David Garrick" by T.W. Robertson, it closed down as the building had become obsolete. It was rebuilt at a cost of £50,000 and re-opened on the 16th December 1904 when the curtain rose on the panto-mime "Babes in the Wood". Seating capacity was now 2,200.

Mr. W.R. Young was the scenic artist at the end of the 19th. century.

In 1908 the Managing Director was Tom B. Davis, Acting Manager was Philip Rodway. On the 1st March 1909 Mr. Rodway was appointed General Manager.

In 1910 Mr. Rodway organised Picture Matinees on Tuesday, Wednesday, Fridays and Saturdays 12.00 noon to 5.00 p.m. Admission 1/0 and 6d.

During the 1914-18 War over 30,000 wounded soldiers were entertained here, free of charge.

It closed on Saturday 15th December 1956 with the showing of the musical "The Fol-de-Rols". It was a very sad occasion.

The Woolworth Building now stands on this site. This is correct, the entire block is called The Woolworth Building, it is a block of offices and retail shops.

The Theatre Royal, New Street, Birmingham.

Medallions of Garrick and Shakespeare, from the Theatre Royal and now on display in the Birmingham Central Library.

THEATRE ROYAL, BIRMINGHAM.

FOR THIS NIGHT ONLY, BLACK-EY'D SUSAN & SIX DEGREES OF CRIME.

FOR THE BENEFIT OF
MR. J. HUDSON
KIRBY

LAST APPEARANCE, and first and only Night of his original American Drama, called

6 DEGREES OF CRIME!

The extraordinary Effect produced by the Representation of this Piece, in all the principal Theatres in America and London, is perhaps unprecedented— **Mr. J. HUDSON KIRBY** having sustained the Character of **Julio** upwards of **SIX HUNDRED NIGHTS!!** This novel and impressive Drama is divided into **SIX PARTS OF DISTINCT ACTION**, representing the progress of Crime, generating from Idleness, dissolute Companions, and graduating through successive Steps up the **LADDER OF CRIME**, to its inevitable termination, amid the **HORRORS OF THE SCAFFOLD**. Its Moral tendency, and Lesson it so strongly inculcates, must ———————— ——— and scrupulous on Dramatic Representations, and tend to prove, if proof ——— ———————, ——— ——— ——— Stage, when properly conducted, is the **VEHICLE OF INSTRUCTION TO ALL.**

LAST APPEARANCE BUT ONE OF

MONS. PLEGE
ON THE TIGHT ROPE.

THURSDAY, APRIL 23rd, 1846,

Will be presented **DOUGLAS JERROLD**'s Celebrated Drama of

BLACK-EY'D SUSAN

OR, "ALL IN THE DOWNS."

William, ... Mr. J. HUDSON KIRBY.

The Admiral,...................................Mr. BARTON	Seaweed,...................................Mr. MORRISS
Captain Crosstree,..............................Mr. KING	Ploughshare,.................................Mr. ROUSE
Doggrass,......................................Mr. G. COOKE	Gnatbrain,...................................Mr. H. WEBB
Hatchet,..Mr. SWINBOURN	Jacob Twig,..................................Mr. ATKINS
Raker,..Mr. VAUDRAY	Blue Peter,..................................Mr. TERRY
Lieutenant Pike,...............................Mr. BURCHELL	Black-Ey'd Susan,............................Miss COVENEY
Quid,..Mr. LEMMON	Dolly Mayflower,.......Miss KATHLEEN FITZWILLIAM

ACT 1, SCENE 1.—A VIEW OF THE COUNTRY IN THE VICINITY OF DEAL.
Honest Gnatbrain's Catechism to the flinty-hearted Doggrass—The Rebuke.
SCENE 2.—A STREET IN THE TOWN OF DEAL. SCENE 3.—SUSAN'S COTTAGE.
Susan's Despair at the Absence of William, and fast approaching Poverty—The Uncle's determination to seize—Arrival of his Factotum—A broken Head—The Man of Law left in Possession—A Novel Writ of Ejectment—Lovers' Quarrels. Scene 5.

VIEW OF THE DOWNS,
THE FLEET AT ANCHOR.
Ships of War, Cutters, &c. Boats will leave the Ships and proceed to Shore. Every arrangement is made to render this a completely **ANIMATED PICTURE**, and impart to it a **PANORAMIC EFFECT.**
LANDING OF WILLIAM AND SAILORS. Scene 6.—MEETING OF WILLIAM AND SUSAN. Scene 7.—A RUSTIC VIEW NEAR DEAL.

BALLAD.—"BLACK-EY'D SUSAN,".........................Mr. TERRY.
GRAND NATIONAL FLAG HORNPIPE, BY MR. & MRS. J. RIDGWAY.
Meeting of Susan and Captain Crosstree—Susan's Cries for Help reach the ears of William, who rushes on, and **CUTS DOWN HIS SUPERIOR OFFICER! TABLEAU, AND END OF ACT 1.**

Act 2, Scene 2.—STATE CABIN of a SHIP of WAR.—THE COURT MARTIAL.
Examination of Witnesses, and WILLIAM's DEFENCE in arrest of Judgment—He is found Guilty, and the Sentence! DEATH! Scene 3.—THE GUN ROOM OF THE SHIP. William takes a Farewell of his Messmates, and presents them with Tokens of Remembrance—Interview between William and Susan. Scene 5.—THE QUARTER-DECK AND POOP OF A SHIP OF WAR. Procession to the Place of Execution, and Conclusion of the Drama.

MONS. PLEGE & HIS TWO SONS
WILL GO THROUGH THEIR GREAT
TIGHT ROPE EXPLOITS!
INTRODUCING VARIOUS NEW AND EXTRAORDINARY EXERCISES.

To conclude with (first and only time) an original American Play in 6 Acts, thrilling, impressive, and ———— ————

Theatre Royal, Birmingham.

October 1885

—:o:—

ENGAGEMENT for SIX NIGHTS of Miss VIVIENNE DALLAS and her LONDON COMPANY of 40 Artistes in Herr Von Suppé's Comic Opera, played 500 nights at the Comedy Theatre,

"BOCCACCIO."

———

Doors open 7 ; extra doors 6.30.   Box Office, 11 till 3.

———

On MONDAY NEXT, MISS WALLIS and her SHAKESPEREAN COMPANY.

Repertoire: "LADY OF LYONS," "ROMEO AND JULIET," "MUCH ADO ABOUT NOTHING," "MEASURE FOR MEASURE," and "AS YOU LIKE IT."

Foyer

THEATRE ROYAL, BIRMINGHAM.

Mr. PHILIP RODWAY takes his Annual Benefit on Monday, March 12th, 1906, when a galaxy of Stars will give their services.

Philip Rodway was born on 21 October 1876 — Trafalgar Day — in Aston Hall, Aston, which was not then part of Birmingham. His father, Alfred Rodway, was the resident curator at the hall. He was a true man of the theatre and a distinguished citizen of Birmingham.

Reproduced from "The Midlander" June 1930.

Theatre interior just prior
to demolition in 1956.

Theatre Royal, Birmingham.

Under the Management of Mr. MERCER H. SIMPSON.

SATURDAY, APRIL 20, & MONDAY, APRIL 22, 1889, & DURING THE WEEK,

At 7.30, Dion Boucicault's Great Drama,—THE

POOR OF BIRMINGHAM.

NEW LOCAL SCENERY BY MR. JOHN JOHNSTONE.

The Prologue. Part First.

Captain Fairweather		Mr. G. H. LEONARD
Mr. Crawley	(a Banker)	Mr. ARTHUR LYLE
Badger	(his Clerk)	Mr. G. H. MACDERMOTT
Edwards	(a Clerk)	Mr. H. MOTLEY

FIFTEEN YEARS are supposed to elapse between the FIRST PART and the SECOND.

The Drama, Part Second.

Badger		Mr. G. H. MACDERMOTT
Paul Fairweather	(a Baker)	Mr. G. H. LEONARD
Puffy	(his Son)	Mr. CHARLES STEYNE
Dan	(a Banker)	Mr. HARRY FISCHER
Mr. Crawley		Mr. ARTHUR LYLE
Mark Livingstone		Mr. J. F. GRAHAM
Edwards		Mr. H. MOTLEY
James		Mr. GEORGE HARDING
Mildew & Binks	(Sheriff's Officers)	Messrs. R. HOSKINS & C. STOKES
Mr. Jones		Mr. W. E. LANE
Policeman		Mr. WATTS
Paddy Hoolan	(an Irish Porter)	Mr. F. BRAYLEY
Lucy Fairweather		Miss E. HERBERT
Alida Crawley		Miss ANNIE BENTLEY
Mrs. Puffy		Mrs. J. C. SMITH

Scene 1.—Mr. Puffy's Shop. Scene 3.—Crawley's Office.
Scene 2.—The Orphan's Garret.
Scene 4.—The Drawing Room in Crawley's Villa, at Edgbaston.

Part Third.

The Town Hall and Council House.

Scene 2.—Exterior of the Theatre Royal. Scene 3—Garrets in Livery Street.

Part Fourth.

Scene 1.—Paul Fairweather's Lodgings. Scene 2—A House in Livery Street.

A HOUSE ON FIRE!

MONDAY, April 29, for Six Nights Only,

MISS KATE VAUGHAN

And her SPECIALLY SELECTED COMPANY, in the Comedy Drama,

"LOVE AND HONOUR," and "HOW IT HAPPENED."

Theatre male staff in January 1902,
taken in the Gallery Yard.

On the 23rd September 1907 the comic opera, 'TOM JONES', by Alexander M. Thompson and Robert Courtneidge, was performed, Harry Welchman played Tom Jones, Ruth Vincent played Sophia and Carrie Moore played Honour, Maid to Sophia.

Miss Carrie Moore,
who plays Honour, Maid to Sophia.

Mr. Harry Welchman,
who plays Tom Jones.

Miss Ruth Vincent

6

BIRMINGHAM
Theatre Royal

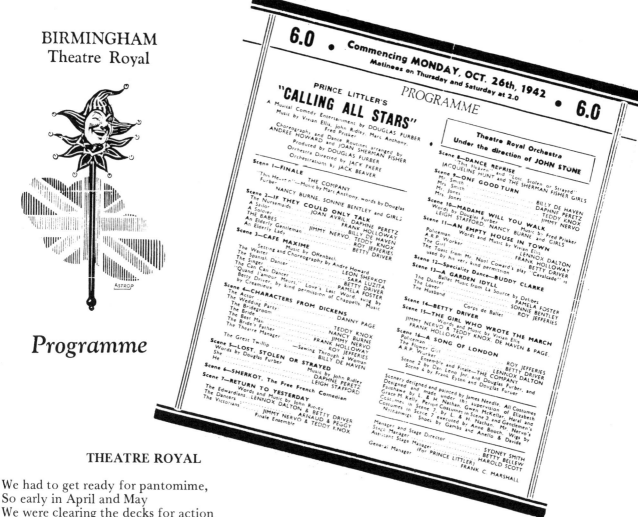

Astrop

Programme

6.0 · Commencing MONDAY, OCT. 26th, 1942 · 6.0
Matinees on Thursday and Saturday at 2.0
PROGRAMME

PRINCE LITTLER'S
"CALLING ALL STARS"
A Musical Comedy Entertainment by DOUGLAS FURBER
Music by Vivian Ellis, John Ridley, Marc Anthony,
Fred Prisker
Choreography and Dance Routines arranged by
ANDREE HOWARD and JOAN SHERMAN FISHER
Produced by DOUGLAS FURBER
Orchestra Directed by JACK PRERE
Orchestrations by JACK BEAVER

Theatre Royal Orchestra
Under the direction of JOHN STONE

THEATRE ROYAL

We had to get ready for pantomime,
So early in April and May
We were clearing the decks for action
And the work that was coming our way.

There were dozens of outfits to make up,
Dresses and millinery too,
Pairs of shoes, near 400 in number
To be coloured in red, green and blue.
There were buttons and sequins and pom-poms
Ribbons and laces galore,
Materials for dresses in satin and velvet
All rainbow colours and more.

We learned all the songs of the 'Panto'
We could hear them rehearsing all day,
They were so nice to hear, and the words were all clear
Not a bit like the junk of today.
One day I dressed up in a chorus girl's togs
(We were not little angels, you know)
Then I whistled and sang in true Panto style
And was offered a part in the show.

But I only liked the dressmaking,
The painting and dyeing of shoes,
One had something to see and be proud of,
So that is the job I would choose.

We worked many hours, the work tedious,
But we all did our bit with a smile,
And when "Phillip Rodway" said Thank-you, well done,
We knew it had all been worth-while.

They were Happy days, and lovely memories.

G. Mg. Lee.

Gladys Lee was a wardrobe mistress at the
Theatre Royal and helped out at the Prince of
Wales Theatre and at Emile Littler's business at
Pantomime House in Oozells Street in the
1920's and '30's.

Derek Salberg standing outside the new entrance in Queensway.

This photograph, taken c 1910, shows the main entrance when it was in John Bright Street, this was the tram route from Navigation Street to the Lickey Hills & Selly Oak and the 33 tram to Ladywood, this turned right at the end of this street and proceeded up Holloway Head to Five Ways and Icknield Port Road terminus.

THE ALEXANDRA THEATRE, John Bright/Station Street

The theatre was opened on Whit Monday 27th May 1901 at a cost of £10,000, it was known as 'The Lyceum' — Lessee and Manager William Coutts. The assistant manager was Albert H. Clarke, Musical Director — Luke Corfield, Acting and Front of House manager — Edward Porter, Stage Manager — Harry Dornton. The Architects Owen and Ward. A Company was formed Coutts Theatre (Birmingham) Limited. The play selected was a Frank Harvey's drama entitled 'The Workman'. For several months he engaged a well known actor of the period H.A. Sainsbury who took the main parts in numerous plays, he was paid £10.00 per week. He left the company in August 1901, after this the fortunes of the theatre deteriorated. A Touring Company then put on a variety of shows, the first performance being 'Cinderella' with Lottie Holland as first Principal Boy. All types of Productions were tried but all in vain. The theatre finally closed in November 1902. Prices of admission then were 2d to 1s, Boxes for 6 — 5s. There were twice nightly performances.

On the 22nd December 1902 it was taken over by Lester Collingwood, he purchased it for £4,450 and he re-named it the 'Alexandra Theatre' after Queen Alexandra. The first performance was a melodrama by Theodore Kremer entitled 'The Fatal Wedding'. He owned and ran the theatre until the 19th of September 1910 when he was killed in his own motor car. He was good natured, generous, smart and had an attractive personality. He organised staff outings for his employees. The theatre was open all the year round. At Christmas 1903 he put on the pantomime 'Aladdin' for 8 weeks. Principal Boy — Minnie Jeffs and Rixie Toole was Principal girl.

Leon Salberg took over the theatre in 1911 in association with his two brothers-in-law Joshia and Julius Thomas. Miss Powell was his Secretary, Herbert Barnes was the Musical Director and W. Steele Jones Stage Manager. In December of this year he put on the pantomime 'Mother Goose'. On the 28th March 1927 he formed the Alexandra Repertory Company giving twice nightly performances and a play a week, this was discontinued from 1974. The theatre was rebuilt in 1935 at a cost of £40,000. Leon died, at the theatre during the performance of "Devonshire Cream" on the 27th of September 1938. He was a modest likeable gentleman.

The running of the theatre was then taken over by his son, Derek Salberg at the age of 25, who commenced his theatrical career at this theatre in 1931. He was director of the theatre until he retired on the 31st July 1977. Michael Bullock then took over and was the director and licensee until 1986. He was then succeeded by the present general manager, Steven Robinson. In 1968, owing to city centre re-development, the entrance to the theatre was extended on to the Queensway.

In March 1974 a £1 million pound appeal fund was arranged, a special luncheon was hosted by the then Lord Mayor, Councillor Bill Sowton, who, besides being a director of the theatre was also on the appeal committee. Mr. Riber Oulsman was the Alexandra Chairman at the time. The appeal was for certain major repairs that were needed to maintain the theatre.

9

Mr. Lester Collingwood's 4th Alexandra staff outing in July 1907. They journed to Worcester by train and then by steamboat to Holt Fleet up the river Severn.

Mr. Lester Collingwood

William Coutts

Leon Salberg

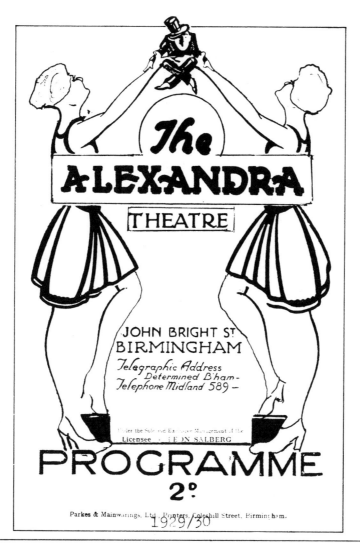

The ALEXANDRA THEATRE

JOHN BRIGHT ST BIRMINGHAM

Telegraphic Address
Determined B'ham —
Telephone Midland 589 —

Under the Sole and Exclusive Management of the
Licensee — LEON SALBERG

PROGRAMME
2º

Parkes & Mainwarings, Ltd., Printers, Coleshill Street, Birmingham.

1929/30

11

"ARMY OF PRE-OCCUPATION"

(Characters in order of their appearance :

"Lucky" Morgan	LARRY NOBLE
Michael Tone	CHARLES MARDEL
Sergeant Gage, R.A.C.	PHILIP STAINTON
Guy Francis Levered	HUGH KELLY
Alan Byssche Wilkinson	JOHN COSHAM
Horace Gregory	BERTRAM DENCH
Penelope Raymond	VANDA GODSELL
Pat Thompson	BETTY BISSETT
Captain Percy, R.A.C.	VERNON FORTESCUE
Gloria Dennis	IRIS RUSSELL
Major Stack	WILLIAM SENIOR
1st German	HENRY RAYNOR
2nd German	RONALD REEVES

Synopsis of Scenery :

ACT I		Takes place in an Army hut
Scene 1		9.55 p.m., November 20th, 1940
		Time Marches On
Scene 2		8.55 a.m., January 1st, 1941

ACT II—Takes place in the grooms' quarters of a deserted country house on the South-East coast of England

Scene 1		5.30 p.m., February 1st, 1941
Scene 2		Shortly after Midnight, February 2nd, 1941

ACT III—The Same. Time : 7 a.m., February 22nd, 1941.

The song in Act I Composed by ERIC LE FERN

Scenery designed by Elisabeth Dorrity

Oil Paintings and Fittings by D. & M. Davis, 3. Livery Street
Furniture by Maples & Co., Ltd., Corporation Street. Antique furnishings, Ornaments, etc., by Frank Hayes, 129, Broad Street. Pictures and Pottery, Hudson Galleries, Great Western Arcade. Glass and China Downie and Grainger, Broad Street. Furs, Faulks Furriers, Islington Row. Silver and Antiques, Julius Brookes, Lower Temple Street. Books, Hector's Book Shop, John Bright St.

In accordance with the requirements of the Licensing Justices—
(a) The public may leave at the end of the performance by all exits and entrances other than those used as queue waiting-rooms, and the doors of such entrance and exits should at that time be open
(b) All gangways, passages and staircases shall be kept entirely free from chairs and other obstructions
(c) Persons shall not be permitted to stand or sit in any part of the intersecting gangways. If standing be permitted at the rear of the seating, sufficient space shall be left for persons to pass easily to and fro
(d) The fireproof curtain shall at all times be maintained in working order and shall be lowered at the beginning and during the time of every performance

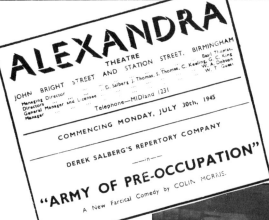

A scene from "Army of Pre-occupation"

this was later renamed "Reluctant Heroes" and was presented at the Whitehall Theatre in London in September 1950.

12

December 24th   For a season until   MARCH 6th.

DEREK SALBERG'S
1964/5 PANTOMIME

JACK AND THE BEANSTALK

THE PREMIER NATIONAL VOCAL TRIO

THE BACHELORS

The most daring and darling Principal Boy

JOY TURPIN

The tallest giant of all   The Skeletons in our cupboard

NICHOLAS BRENT   **LES OSCARS**

The celebrated colourful "card" and capable comedian

COLIN CROMPTON

The gold-medal cycling   The most mysterious and
champions   magical

THE RENELLIS   **GEORGE CAMPO**
                  assisted by Lina Marvell

The Magnificent Mistress   The most regal "royal" and
of Melody   masterful monarch

PAMELA PENFOLD   **ALLEN CHRISTIE**

The fabulous favourite fairy   The Most Loveable

ANN SHEPHARD   **LEHMISKI LADIES**

The Ever-ready

JONATHON EVERETT

and

The most splendid comical acrobatic dancing dame

JACK TRIPP

1901-1951

ALEXANDRA
THEATRE
BIRMINGHAM

Golden Jubilee
Production

THE SCHOOL
FOR SCANDAL

BY

RICHARD BRINSLEY SHERIDAN

MAY 21st TO JUNE 2nd 1951

ALEXANDRA THEATRE BIRMINGHAM

Managing Director and Licensee - DEREK SALBERG   General Manager: W. A. DOBSON
Directors: MRS. S. THOMAS, C. KEELING, MRS. M. THOMAS
EDMUND H. KING, DAVID F. WISEMAN
Secretary: C. WOOLRIDGE.   Assistant Manager: GORDON PRICE
Publicity: LAWSON TROUT PUBLICITY LTD.
Box Office (MRS. SIDDONS) open 10 a.m.—7-15 p.m.
Telephones: MID. 1231/2/3.   Office: MID. 5536.   Stage Door: MID. 3180

EVENINGS AT 7-0 p.m.   **MATINEES AT 2-30 p.m.**

PUSS IN BOOTS

The Characters in the Pantomime:

COBBLER	WILLIAM AVENELL
TIMMY, THE CAT	KATHLEEN ALLWOOD
FAIRY	JOAN ROSS
MILL HANDS	3 GRAHAM BROTHERS
SIMON	NORMAN VAUGHAN
BARONESS	GEORGE LACY
JACK	DENNIS LOTIS
PRINCESS VALENTINA	CHRISTINE YATES
KING	DEREK ROYLE
WICKED WIZARD'S MOTHER	KATHLEEN ST. JOHN
JOE	TERRY HALL
PUSS IN BOOTS	DAPHNE DE WIT
WICKED WIZARD	WILLIAM AVENELL
WATCHMEN, BARKERS, COACHMEN, etc.	MASTERSINGERS

MICHAEL JORDAN, HERBERT CARSON. ALASTAIR DICK
JOHN MURPHY, REG GREY, NEIL MACLEAN.

VILLAGERS, SERVING MAIDS, etc.   LEHMISKI LADIES

PATRICIA COTTRELL (HEAD GIRL), JUDY SEARBY, BARBARA
THORNTON, JANIS THOMAS, ELAINE NOAD, MARGARET SANDERS,
MARY TANSER, GILLIAN TANDY, KATHLEEN ALLWOOD, SHEILA
JEFFRIES, VALERIE MARSHALL, CHRISTINE HUTCHINSON, MAVIS
MECHAM, JANET TARRANT, ANN BENNETT, VANESSA LATOUR,
BILLIE WHATLEY.

1958-59

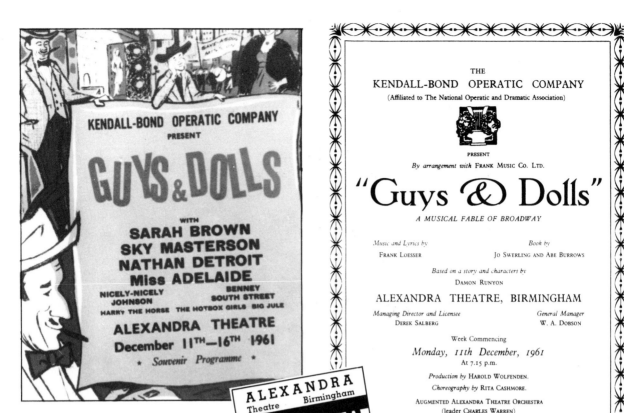

THE
KENDALL-BOND OPERATIC COMPANY
(Affiliated to The National Operatic and Dramatic Association)

PRESENT

By arrangement with FRANK MUSIC CO. LTD.

"Guys & Dolls"
A MUSICAL FABLE OF BROADWAY

Music and Lyrics by	*Book by*
FRANK LOESSER	JO SWERLING and ABE BURROWS

Based on a story and characters by
DAMON RUNYON

ALEXANDRA THEATRE, BIRMINGHAM

Managing Director and Licensee	*General Manager*
DEREK SALBERG	W. A. DOBSON

Week Commencing
Monday, 11th December, 1961
At 7.15 p.m.

Production by HAROLD WOLFENDEN.
Choreography by RITA CASHMORE.

AUGMENTED ALEXANDRA THEATRE ORCHESTRA
(leader CHARLES WARREN)
under the direction of JACK MYERS.

ALEXANDRA
Theatre Birmingham
DEC. 16
SAT. 1st PERF. 4-45
STALLS 8/-
E19
No Tickets exchanged or returned

═══ "GUYS & DOLLS" ═══

CHARACTERS IN ORDER OF APPEARANCE	
NICELY-NICELY JOHNSON	FRANK PEMBERTON
BENNY SOUTHSTREET	FRANK DAVIS
RUSTY CHARLIE	JOHN HEMMS
SARAH BROWN	PAMELA READ
ARVIDE ABERNATHY	KEITH CHATERIS
AGATHA	MILDRED DAVIES
HARRY THE HORSE	KEITH KNOTT
LIEUTENANT BRANNIGAN	IVOR GORNAL
NATHAN DETROIT	HAROLD WOLFENDON
ANGIE THE OX	WALTER LANE
MISS ADELAIDE	ANNEMARIE MYERS
SKY MASTERSTON	STANLEY PHILLIPS
MIMI	MYRA PHILLIPS
GENERAL MATILDA B. CARTWRIGHT	BETTY WEATHERHOGG
SOCIETY MAX	JIM KELSEY
BIG JULE	GORDON CARTER
BRANDY BOTTLE BATES	JOHN BERRY
HOT BOX ANNOUNCER	JOHN ROCHELLE
MISSION BAND	ANDREW SILVER PAUL SLEIGH PAUL CHILDS

SPECIALITY DANCERS
JACKIE ASKEW, PAT READ, GERRARD HUNT.

HOT BOX GIRLS
JACKIE ASKEW, SYLVIA BOWEN, KATHLEEN CHURCHILL, BETTY DARKES, IRENE DAVIS, ELSIE JOHNSON, ANN MCKENZIE, MYRA PHILLIPS, PAT READ, CAROLE ROBERTS, ANN SMITH, SHIRLEY TURNER.

DOLLS AND CUBANO GIRLS
DOROTHY DARKES, MONICA DEAN, VALERIE FELTON, JOSEPHINE HUGHES, BARBARA HUTTON, JOYCE TIPPING.

MISSION GIRLS
NORAH STIRKE, ALICE BILLINGTON, JOYCE TIPPING, GLADYS HOLLIDAY.

GUYS, CRAP SHOOTERS AND CUBANO BOYS
BARRY ALBERT, JIM ASKEW, TREVOR BAUM, JOHN BERRY, GERALD FELTON, GERRARD HUNT, CHARLIE JACKSON, FRANK JEANES, JIM KELSEY, JOHN MITCHELL, DOUGLAS READ, JOHN ROCHELLE, JOE STOWE, JOHN TAYLOR, LEN WILSON.

SYNOPSIS OF SCENES

ACT I

Scene	1	Broadway
Scene	2	Interior of the Save-a-Soul Mission
Scene	3	A Phone Booth
Scene	4	The Hot Box, Nightclub
Scene	5	A street off Broadway
Scene	6	Exterior of the Mission. Noon the next day
Scene	7	A street off Broadway
Scene	8	Havana, Cuba—El Cafe Cubano
Scene	9	Outside El Cafe Cubano. Immediately following
Scene	10	Exterior of the Mission

ACT II

Scene	1	The Hot Box, Nightclub
Scene	2	Forty-Eighth Street
Scene	3	Crap Game in the Sewer
Scene	4	A street off Broadway
Scene	5	Interior of the Save-a-Soul Mission
Scene	6	Near Times Square
Scene	7	Broadway

(Interval of 15 minutes between Acts I and II)

CREDITS

Hon. Treasurer	GEORGE BRAMLEY
Stage Manager for Alexandra Theatre	FRED REEVES
Stage Manager for Kendall-Bond Company	ERNEST THORNEWELL
Electrician	ALAN CHESTER
Box Office Manageress	MRS. E. M. SIDDONS
Wardrobe	EDNA CORBETT DOROTHY DARKES
Scenery	JAMES FREDERICKS, WESTON-S-MARE
Costumes	MORRIS ANGEL & SON LTD., LONDON
Additional Properties	EMPIRE STUDIOS, SMETHWICK
Accompanist	WILLIAM COX

Our thanks to A. W. North, Esq., and R. J. C. Favill, Esq., of Wheelers Lane Boy's Secondary School, for co-operation and training of boys in the Mission Band. Petite the Poodle appears by kind permission of Mrs. Harry Sessions.

A NIGHT WITH THE STARS

A TRIBUTE TO

DEREK SALBERG

Sunday 24th July, 1977

★ ★ ★ ★ ★

Artistes appearing will include:

JOHN ALDERTON	TERRY HALL &
AVRIL ANGERS	LENNY THE LION
ARTHUR ASKEY	FRANK IFIELD
MAXINE AUDLEY	GEORGE LACY
JEAN BAYLESS	PAT LANCASTER
BRENDA BRUCE	LEO MAGUIRE
PATRICK CARGILL	JUDY PARFITT
ALLEN CHRISTIE	SANDY POWELL
LESLIE CROWTHER	DEREK ROYLE
JIM DAVIDSON	TONY STEEDMAN
BETTY FOX	CHARLIE STEWART
MODERN GENERATION	DAVID TOMLINSON
RAYMOND FRANCIS	JACK TRIPP
PHILIP GARSTON-JONES	LESLIE WELCH
PETER GOODWRIGHT	GEORGIE WOOD
NOELE GORDON	HARRY WORTH

also other artistes too late for inclusion in the programme

★ ★ ★ ★ ★

Musical Director: PETER DAY

Production under the direction of ALAN CURTIS

Gala devised by MICHAEL BULLOCK

───── *Please do not smoke whilst the curtain is up* ─────

We would like to thank the Artistes, Stage Management and Orchestra - without whose generosity and assistance this Gala would not have been possible.

Stage Management - **ROY ASTLEY**
ALAN WHITE
LIZ STERN
HEATHER McCONACHIE

Public Relations - **MALCOLM FARQUHAR**

Orchestra - **TREVOR CHARLTON, TREVOR OERTON, STAN POOLE, ARTHUR ROBERTS, GEOFF SMITH, JIMMY WEDGE**

Resident Stage Manager - **RICHARD TURNER**

Chief Electrician - **ERIC OTTO**

The above was correct at the time of going to press

The following artistes were prevented from appearing by professional commitments, but send their best wishes to Derek and for the success of this evening:

THE BACHELORS, THE BARRON KNIGHTS, TONY BRITTON, ROY CASTLE, RONNIE CORBETT, LES DAWSON, MICHAEL DENISON, REG DIXON, KEN DODD, VAL DOONICAN, CYRIL FLETCHER, DULCIE GRAY, THE GRUMBLEWEEDS, JOHN HANSON, BERNARD HEPTON, TREVOR HOWARD, TEDDY JOHNSON & PEARL CARR, ARTHUR LOWE, ALFRED MARKS, JOHN LE MESURIER, KENNETH MORE, PEGGY MOUNT, ANNA NEAGLE, DES O'CONNOR, LYNETTE RAE, BERYL REID, TED ROGERS, LEONARD ROSSITER, LESLIE SANDS, JIMMY TARBUCK, NORMAN VAUGHAN, MIKE & BERNIE WINTERS, NORMAN WISDOM, GLYN WORSNIP.

Brochure researched and compiled by **Jackie Swancutt** and **Alan Davies**.
Edited by **Michael Bullock**

No Cameras or Tape Recorders allowed in the auditorium

Two pages from the author's farewell Gala Night programme are reproduced above and on the page opposite.

Frank Ifield, Judy Parfitt and Harry Worth were, due to various circumstances, unable to appear, but Marius Goring and Ray Paul, though not listed above, were welcome additions to the artistes.

Alexandra Theatre

BOARD OF DIRECTORS: Councillor BERNARD ZISSMAN (Chairman)
Councillor Mrs. THELMA COOKE, ED DOOLAN, Councillor HUGH McCALLION, Don MacLEAN
ROBERT M OULSNAM, JOHN M.B. OWEN, JOHN SEVER, Hon Ald GERRY R. SIMMONS O.B.E
REGINALD WALL, F.C.A.
General Manager: STEPHEN ROBINSON
Theatre Manager and Licensee: ANTHONY PUGH, Press and PR Officer: PAUL GREENFIELD
Financial Controller: PAUL HAYWARD, Box Office Manageress: ANGELA HARRIS
Box Office 021-643 1231, Administration 021-643 5536, Stage Door 021 643 3180
The Board of Directors gratefully acknowledge financial assistance from THE BIRMINGHAM CITY COUNCIL

July 1987

COMMENCING 1 JULY 1987

BRIAN HEWITT-JONES, CHRIS MORENO
and PAUL ELLIOTT present

CONSTANCE CUMMINGS
DAVID GRIFFIN

by
ROYCE RYTON

with
KATHLEEN BYRON

GARY HOPE	CELESTINE RANDALL	MORAR KENNEDY	ELIZABETH ALEXANDER	VERNON HOUGH

ANITA CAREY
and
MICHAEL COCHRANE

Designed by	*Directed by*	*Lighting by*
TERRY PARSONS	ROGER REDFARN	NICK CHELTON

ARTS COUNCIL FUNDED
A THEATRE ROYAL PLYMOUTH PRODUCTION

SMOKING IS PROHIBITED IN THE AUDITORIUM
The Management reserve the right to refuse admission to this theatre and to change, vary or omit,
without previous notice, any item in the programme.
FIRST AID facilities are provided by St. John Ambulance members who give their services voluntarily
THE USE OF CAMERAS OR TAPE RECORDERS IN THIS THEATRE IS FORBIDDEN
Please do not distract other patrons by rustling sweet papers.

BY ROYCE RYTON

CAST, IN ORDER OF APPEARANCE

Mabell, Countess of Airlie	KATHLEEN BYRON
Queen Mary	CONSTANCE CUMMINGS
The Hon. Margaret Wyndham	MORAR KENNEDY
Queen's Page (John)	VERNON HOUGH
King Edward VIII (David)	DAVID GRIFFIN
The Princess Royal (Mary)	CELESTINE RANDALL
The Duchess of Gloucester (Alice)	ELIZABETH ALEXANDER
Walter Monckton, K.C.	GARY HOPE
The Duke of York (Bertie)	MICHAEL COCHRANE
The Duchess of York (Elizabeth)	ANITA CAREY

Directed by	ROGER REDFARN
Designed by	TERRY PARSONS
Lighting by	NICK CHELTON

FOR THE CROWN MATRIMONIAL COMPANY

Company Stage Manager	VERNON HOUGH
Deputy Stage Manager	PHIL JOLLY
Assistant Stage Managers	MARK PHILLIPS
	PAMELA HARDMAN
Wardrobe Mistress	SARA DYER

FOR E & B PRODUCTIONS (THEATRE) LTD.

Directors	PAUL ELLIOTT
	BRIAN HEWITT-JONES
	CHRIS MORENO
Production Associate	RHONDA HASLAM
Production Secretary	JACQUIE HARTHILL
Production Assistant	DEBBIE BRINKMAN

FOR THEATRE ROYAL PLYMOUTH

General Manager	ANDREW WELCH
Artistic Director	ROGER REDFARN

PRODUCTION ACKNOWLEDGEMENTS

Sets and Properties built and painted by Theatre Royal Plymouth Workshop; costumes made in the Theatre Royal Plymouth Wardrobe Department.

CROWN MATRIMONIAL © Royce Ryton 1972. Copyright agent for the play — Michael Imison Playwrights Ltd., 28 Almeida Street, London N1 1TD. Tel: 01-354 3174

The action takes place in the late summer, autumn and winter of 1936. The last scene takes place in the autumn of 1945.
The setting is Queen Mary's private sitting room on the first floor of Marlborough House, London.
There will be one interval of 15 minutes.

ACT ONE	ACT TWO
1. September 1936, late morning	1. Early December 1936, late morning
2. November, early evening	2. A few days later, late evening
3. Later, the same evening	3. Later, the same week, early evening
	4. Autumn 1945, afternoon

1987

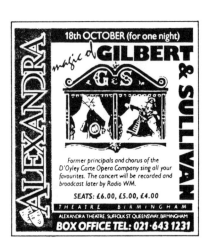

ALEXANDRA
THEATRE · BIRMINGHAM

1987

16

PRINCE OF WALES THEATRE, Broad Street

The theatre was officially opened on the 3rd September 1856 at a cost of £12,000. The production chosen was, "The Messiah". The theatre was then known as "The Birmingham Music Hall".

In 1861 Charles Dickens appeared there and gave a reading of his Christmas Carol. In 1862 the proprietor James Scott applied for a dramatic licence, later in that year he sold the theatre to W.H. Swanborough, he changed the name to "Prince of Wales Operetta House", in honour of the marriage of the then Prince of Wales, Edward VII (1841-1910) but, in 1865 the words Operetta House were discarded. In 1866 James Rodgers became the Lessee, he spent thousands of pounds on building and enlarging the theatre. In 1879 he brought his son, who, until then had been a Captain in the Merchant Navy, into the theatre so that he could take a less active part in its running. He made him joint manager in 1884 although he was the sole proprietor until his death on 6th May 1890 aged 74 years. His son then formed a limited company known as Rodgers Limited. He did considerable refurbishment to the theatre but in 1898 sold it to a syndicate, The Prince of Wales Theatre (Birmingham) Limited who appointed Mr. J.F. Graham as manager. He had been for many years a well known actor. He continued in office until he retired in 1911 (he died on 27th November 1933 aged 82 years). In 1918 Philip Rodway was appointed manager and eventually became Managing Director, he continued in office until his death on the 2nd February 1932 at the early age of 55. He was also the Managing Director of the Theatre Royal in New Street which was his real love. The new manager was then appointed Harry Rushworth. Emile Littler the well known theatrical personality was invited to join the board of directors in 1935. He did his best to revive the fortunes of the theatre and re-introduced pantomimes. He was then appointed Chairman and Licensee, Managers — Howard & Wyndham Ltd. Managing Director A. Stewart Cruikshank, Manager — J.G. Stewart. On the 9th of April 1941 the theatre received a direct hit in one of the first air raids on the city during the last war, this completely destroyed the interior of the theatre. This was a very sad loss to the citizens of Birmingham. What remained of the original building was demolished in 1987 when the new Civic and Conference Centre was being erected over the entire area.

In August 1913 after being closed for the annual holiday period of 2 weeks, which was the normal practice in all theatres at that period, the management put on film shows for the first time in its history, the famous Kinemacolour Pictures, taken by Mr. Charles Urban, of the Royal Durdar at Delhi. This form of entertainment was unique as it introduced to Birmingham the wonders of animated photography in natural colours, to which the blazing light of the Indian sun has done full justice. The following week the programme included pictures of the cutting of the Panama Canal, and scenes from the Balkan wars. The price of admission was considerably reduced for this form of entertainment and was very well patronised.

Prince of Wales Theatre.

October 1879.

February 1888.

April 1880.

31st October 1885.

At the Prince of Wales, Mrs. Langtry pays a return visit
to Birmingham, and we are sorry to say that we cannot see
the improvement we expected in her acting. Possibly we
expected too much from her on account of the old adage
which says "Practice makes perfect," but, anyway, we are
disappointed. The lady is undoubtedly possessed of talent,
but we know plenty of actresses in minor positions who are
equally gifted.
However, if we fail to see the exceptional merits of her
performances, the same cannot be said of the Birmingham
public, whose patronage she cannot complain of. She is
well supported by a first-class company, such actors as Mr.
Coghlan and Mr. Fred Everill being hosts in themselves.

'Press Comments' November 1885.

MISS CHRISTINE SILVER
February 1906.

She played the principal role in the play, "The Lion and the Mouse" by Charles Klein on September 10th 1906.

"BETTY IN MAYFAIR"

Miss Evelyn Laye, who is appearing this week in her "London Success" at the Prince of Wales Theatre, is a lady of many accomplishments. She has a strong, pure, and flexible singing voice; is an actress of real art; has a sense of humour and drollery; dances delightfully; and, as everybody knows, is as pretty as a picture.

The play is good material for her – not only for her, but for others as well; notably for Miss Mary Leigh, Miss Lilian Mason, Mr. Jack Hobbs, Mr. Wilfred Temple, and Mr. Cecil Brooking. Miss Leigh has another singing and dancing part; Mr. Hobbs is a comically bashful lover; and Mr. Brooking does extremely well in the role of a country vicar (congratulations to the author on keeping this vicar in the story throughout, and refusing to "guy" him, but just letting his amiable humour provide its own gentle fun).

As the play develops, bustles and crinolines are seen in profusion, and it was evident that the crowded audience — with the 1926 viewpoint — thought them a great joke.

The music is lively and jovial, if not very distinguished. And the play is valuable, if only as proof that this kind of play can get along without the (supposed) indispensable help of a low comedian. There is not a wilfully red nose in it from start to finish!

W.H.G.

19

PROGRAMME
6th December 1937

PRINCE OF WALES THEATRE
BIRMINGHAM

3D

Prince of Wales Theatre
Birmingham

Telephone · · MIDland 5684 (3 lines)

Proprietors .... THE PRINCE OF WALES THEATRE (BIRMINGHAM) LTD
Chairman & Licensee .... EMILE LITTLER
Managers, HOWARD & WYNDHAM, LTD Managing Director, A. STEWART CRUIKSHANK
Manager .... J. G. STEWART

MONDAY, 6th Dec., 1937, for 6 NIGHTS at 7.30
Reduced Price Matinees Thursday & Saturday at 2.30

Charles Killick

and

Victor Payne-Jennings

present

"SARAH SIMPLE"

A COMEDY IN THREE ACTS

by

A. A. Milne

This new Regency Style Facade was erected in 1986 after a grant of £350,000 was given by the West Midlands County Council just before the council was abolished in June of that year.

Interior of the Theatre 1980/81

Birmingham Hippodrome Hurst Street in 1959

BIRMINGHAM HIPPODROME, corner of Hurst and Inge Street.

When it was officially opened on the 9th October 1899 by Councillor Marsh it was known as the "Tower of Varieties and Circus". Proprietors James and Henry Draysey. Manager Harry Calver. Owing to the very poor public response it closed after only 5 weeks on the 11th November 1899. The following year the building was refurbished and on Monday 20th August 1900 was reopened as the "Tivoli Theatre". Proprietors Harry Fowler Stirling and Thomas Barrasford. Manager Harry Calver. Director and Ring Master R. Roberts. Musical Director E. Davis. It gave two evening performances — 7.00 and 9.00 p.m. Prices of admission, Stalls 2/– (reserved 2/6) Pit 1/–, Gallery 6d. (see copy of opening programme for full details).

In October 1903 it again changed its name, this time to Hippodrome. Proprietors The New Birmingham Hippodrome Ltd. In 1908 the Managing Director was T. Barrasford, Manager H.F. Stirling. Resident Manager, Frank Weston, he was preceded by P.D. Elbourne and the Musical Director was J.D. Rogers, followed by Fred. Leake and W. Crabtree. Mr. Elborne left in 1910 to take up a position with the Palace Theatre, Leicester (see copy of his testimonial). The Manager then appointed was Ben de Frece. Resident Manager and Licensee in 1912 was Harry Hamilton. It closed in 1914 and was re-opened on the 13th February 1917 by its original proprietors the Draysey Bros. It again closed in 1919 and was rebuilt, architects Burdwood & Mitchell and was taken over by Moss Empires Ltd. The Proprietors on the opening programme The Variety Theatres (Birmingham)Ltd. Managing Director Charles Gulliver. Manager Jas. W. Kilgour. The play selected was a revue "Happy Hours!" it was shown on Wednesday 23rd February 1925. Total seating capacity 2,000. In 1929 the Joint Managing Directors were William Evans and C.M. Woolf, Director George Black. Mr. Kilgour was still the manager. Musical Director was Harold Brewer. Later Directors and Manager were Val Parnell, Louis Benjamin, Bert Adams and W. May. The present theatre director is Richard Johnston, Theatre Manager and Licensee Barry Hopson, Stage Director Tony Guest.

In 1979 the theatre freehold was purchased by the City of Birmingham for £50,000 and it was again closed for extensive renovations and alterations. This provided a new stage, orchestra pit and fly-tower, at a cost of over two million pounds. Further improvements were made in 1984 including stage enlargement, air-conditioning, dance studios, rehearsal rooms etc. Seating capacity now 1,943. It is now the English regional base for the Sadler's Wells Royal Ballet and the Welsh National Opera Company.

As a point of interest I should like to mention that in the early 1900's a film projector was installed in the theatre and films shown, (then known as bioscope), after each live performance. This became very popular with patrons, however, when cinemas opened this practice ceased in 1914.

The P. D. Elbourne Testimonial.

As announced in our last issue the reply to our appeal on behalf of Mr. P. D. Elbourne has been such a generous one that the lists were closed on Saturday last, and in deference to the expressed wishes of Mr. Elbourne a cheque for the amount received by *Midland Amusements* was on Sunday, July 10th, handed to Mr. Elbourne and we append a letter and receipt from him below. We take this opportunity of tendering sincere thanks to the supporters and subscribers to this Fund for their generous assistance.

The Palace Theatre, Leicester,
July 10th, 1910.

Received from M. Bernsten, Esq., the sum of £40 10s. 9d. (Forty pounds ten shillings and ninepence) being the amount contributed to the " P. D. Elbourne Testimonial Fund."

With thanks, P. D. ELBOURNE.

The Palace, Leicester,
July 10th, 1910.

M. Bernsten. Esq., *Midland Amusements*, Birmingham.

Dear Mr. Bernsten, – Your letter—with cheque—to hand. Really, I would like to personally thank my many friends for their great generosity and goodness to me and their encouraging wishes for my future success, and I sincerely look forward to meeting them all many, many times again in the near future, meanwhile, I ask you to convey through the medium of your valuable and popular *Midland Amusements* my full and deep appreciation and sincerest thanks for their magnificent send-off, and in conclusion I desire to thank you personally very much for all your extreme kindness displayed on my behalf during my stay in dear old Birmingham. Again thanking you, I remain,

Yours sincerely, P. D. ELBOURNE.

Week Commencing Monday, August 6th, 1934

1 OVERTURE
Selected

---

2 DELFONT & TOKO ...... Eccentric Dancers

---

3 LESLIE SARONY & LESLIE HOLMES
(The Two Leslies) Of B.B.C. Fame

---

4 FORSYTHE, SEAMON & FARRELL
" Get Hot "

---

5 JACK PAYNE WITH HIS BAND
Conductor .... JACK PAYNE

H. POWELL	Violin	J. ROBERTSON	Trumpet
S. WILLIAMS	Violin	S. FEARN	Trumpet
B. EASSON	Violin	J. FULLER	Trombone
J. DUNLOP	Violin	J. JONES	Trombone
S. MILLWARD	Saxophone	C. ASPLIN	Sousaphone
D. STEPHENSON	Saxophone	H. GROVES	String Bass
S. OSBORNE	Saxophone	W. SCOTT-COOMBER	
C. LAMPRECHT	Saxophone		Vocalist and Guitar
P. TRIKS	Saxophone	R. GENARDER	
W. THORBURN	Piano		Vocalist and Banjo
H. BULLIMORE	Trumpet	J. SIMPSON	Drums

---

6 INTERMISSION
SELECTION BY THE HIPPODROME ORCHESTRA
Conducted by HARRY M. PELL

---

7 DELFONT & TOKO Will Again Entertain

Programme continued overleaf

DANCE AT TONY'S

24

THE CHRISTMAS PANTOMIME

ROBINSON CRUSOE

HIPPODROME BIRMINGHAM

PROGRAMME SIXPENCE

TOM ARNOLD presents
IN ITS ENTIRETY THE MAGNIFICENT
LONDON PALLADIUM PANTOMIME PRODUCTION

ROBINSON CRUSOE

★ STARRING ★

DAVID WHITFIELD

in his outstanding characterisation
of 'ROBINSON CRUSOE'
as played by him at the
LONDON PALLADIUM

BOOK NOW — FOR WHAT SURELY MUST BE
THE MIDLANDS MOST LAVISH PANTOMIME

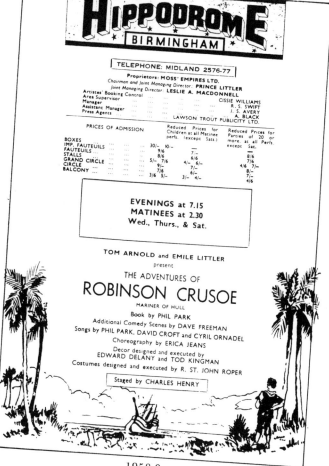

MOSS'
HIPPODROME
BIRMINGHAM

TELEPHONE: MIDLAND 2576-77

Proprietors: MOSS' EMPIRES LTD.
Chairman and Joint Managing Director: PRINCE LITTLER
Joint Managing Director: LESLIE A. MACDONNELL

Artistes' Booking Control
Area Supervisor ... ... CISSIE WILLIAMS
Manager ... ... R. S. SWIFT
Assistant Manager ... ... J. S. AVERY
Press Agents ... ... A. BLACK
LAWSON TROUT PUBLICITY LTD.

PRICES OF ADMISSION			Reduced Prices for Children at all Matinee perfs. (except Sats.)	Reduced Prices for Parties of 20 or more, at all Perfs. except Sat.
BOXES				
IMP. FAUTEUILS ...	30/-	10/-	—	—
FAUTEUILS ...	9/6		7/-	—
STALLS	8/6		6/6	8/6
GRAND CIRCLE ...	5/- 7/6	4/- 6/-	7/6
CIRCLE	9/-		7/-	4/6 7/-
BALCONY ...	7/6		6/-	8/-
	3/6 5/-	3/- 4/-	7/-	4/6

EVENINGS at 7.15
MATINEES at 2.30
Wed., Thurs., & Sat.

TOM ARNOLD and EMILE LITTLER
present

THE ADVENTURES OF
ROBINSON CRUSOE
MARINER OF HULL

Book by PHIL PARK
Additional Comedy Scenes by DAVE FREEMAN
Songs by PHIL PARK, DAVID CROFT and CYRIL ORNADEL
Choreography by ERICA JEANS
Decor designed and executed by
EDWARD DELANY and TOD KINGMAN
Costumes designed and executed by R. ST. JOHN ROPER

Staged by CHARLES HENRY

1958-9

25

Hippodrome · Birmingham

TUESDAY, MAY 29th for 4 weeks
Evenings at 7.15
Weds. and Thurs. and Whit. Mon. June 11th
at 5.0 and 8.0
Saturdays at 1.45, 5.0 and 8.0

LESLIE A. MACDONNELL
announces that

TOM ARNOLD
for Holiday on Ice (Great Britain) Ltd.

presents

An adaptation on ICE
of

The Wizard of OZ

by FRANK L. BAUM

with the original music from the Metro-Goldwyn-Mayer motion picture by
Harold Arlen and E. Y. Harburg
Additional musical numbers by John Taylor
Leo Feist Inc., New York—N.Y. copyright owner and publisher of the music
Presented by special arrangement with
Tam-Witmark Music Library Inc., New York City

Produced and Directed by
GERALD PALMER

Dance and musical numbers staged by ROSS TAYLOR

Scenery and Decor by   Costumes designed by
EDWARD DELANY   ANTHONY HOLLAND

PLEASE NOTE—PHOTOGRAPHING IN THIS THEATRE IS FORBIDDEN
The Management reserves the right to refuse admission to this theatre, and
to change, vary or omit, without previous notice, any items of the programme

1965

Birmingham HIPPODROME

First performance
21 December 1981

LOUIS BENJAMIN presents

DANNY
LA RUE
as the 'MERRY' WIDOW TWANKEY

in

Aladdin

with

DILYS   THE HALFWITS
WATLING
as ALADDIN

BRIAN MARSHALL
as WISHEE WASHEE

DAVID ELLEN
as GENIE OF THE RING

THE HIPPODROME
BOYS & GIRLS

GEORGE REIBBITT   GEORGE GILES

LEON GREENE
as ABANAZAR

DANIELLE CARSON   GUY GREGORY

Directed & Choreographed by
DOUGIE SQUIRES

Book by BRYAN BLACKBURN
Danny La Rue's costumes by MARK CANTER
Costumes designed by CYNTHIA TINGEY
& executed by BERMANS of LONDON
Scenery designed by TOD KINGMAN

1981

Birmingham HIPPODROME

20 - 24 October
BMOS Presents
MY FAIR LADY

26 - 31 October
WINNIE THE POOH
Half Term Holiday

Sunday 1 November
BAD NEWS
are: Rik Mayall,
Ade Edmonson, Nigel Planer
Peter Richardson

2 - 7 November
NEW SADLER'S
WELLS OPERA
H.M.S. PINAFORE

9 - 14 November
SADLER'S WELLS
ROYAL BALLET
La fille, Mal Gardee,
Paramour, Gloriana,
Paquita

17 - 21 November
GLYNDEBOURNE
TOURING OPERA

BOX OFFICE
021 622 7486
OPENS 10AM - 8.30PM.

1987

26

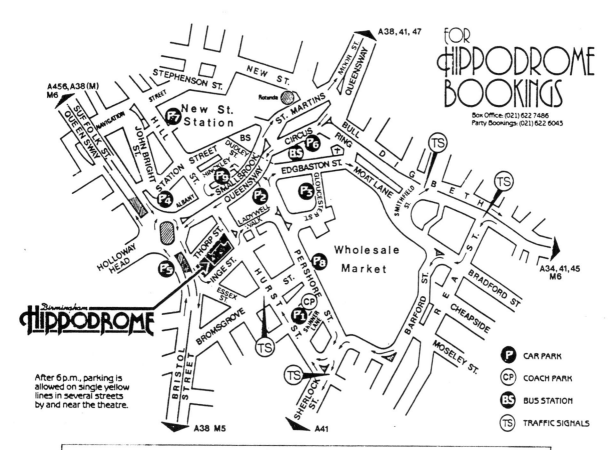

A38, 41, 47

A456, A38 (M) M6

STEPHENSON ST.

NEW ST.

New St. Station

MOOR ST. QUEENSWAY

ST. MARTINS

CIRCUS

BULL RING

DIGBETH

Wholesale Market

A34, 41, 45 M6

BROMSGROVE

HURST ST.

PERSHORE ST.

BRISTOL STREET

A38 M5

A41

SHERLOCK ST.

Birmingham
HIPPODROME

After 6 p.m., parking is
allowed on single yellow
lines in several streets
by and near the theatre.

Ⓟ	CAR PARK
ⓒⓟ	COACH PARK
Ⓑⓢ	BUS STATION
Ⓣⓢ	TRAFFIC SIGNALS

Birmingham
HIPPODROME

Hurst Street, Birmingham B5 4TB

THEATRE INFORMATION

Birmingham Hippodrome Theatre Trust Limited
David G Justham (Chairman)
Timothy D Morris DLMA
Cllr Neville B A Bosworth CBE LLB
Bruce W Tanner
Francis C Graves OBE DL FRICS
Councillor Chris Kirk BSc DIC PhD
B V Smith BSc MBA

Box Office	021-622 7486
Party Bookings	021-622 6043
Administration	021-622 7437
Catering	021-622 4193

Management and Senior Staff

Theatre Director	Richard Johnston
Theatre Manager and Licensee	Barry Hopson
Stage Director	Tony Guest
Finance Manager	Mike Bedward
Box Office Manager	Carol Gardner
Chief Electrician	John Reason
Marketing Manager	Peter Rowell
Press Officer	Roulla Xenides
Bar and Catering Manager	Kim Devey

Box Office
The Box Office is open from 10.00am - 8.30pm Monday - Saturday. Please phone the general line (622 7486) for enquiries and telephone reservations. If your group is for 20 or more then phone our special Party Booking Office on 622 6043. Please check your tickets carefully as once paid for they cannot be exchanged or money refunded. In response to general requests, latecomers cannot be admitted to their seats until a suitable break in the performance.

Special Facilities
Please note that a chair lift from the foyer to stalls level is available for disabled patrons.

We can advise on wheelchair access and positions - please inform the box office if you are booking seats for wheelchairs. An induction loop has been fitted in this theatre for the benefit of hearing aid users.

Interval Refreshments
Coffee and cold drinks are served at the coffee bar in the foyer. For evening performances the bars in the Stalls and Circle are open for interval drinks. Ice cream is available in the foyer or from the usherettes at either side of the Stalls and Circle.

The Hippodrome Shop
The foyer shop is open before and after performances and during the interval, selling a wide range of theatre and 'Ancient Order of Hippos' souvenirs.

Gift Vouchers
Just the ticket for that special present: Mozart or musicals, Shakespeare or super-stars, panto or pas de deux – there's something your friends and relations, clients, staff or customers would love to see. With Hippodrome Gift Vouchers you can give a special night-out to a show of their choice on the night they are free to go. The ideal gift for birthdays, Christmas, Anniversaries, Valentines or Mothers Day. They also provide excellent motivators for purchase and sales force incentives, competition prizes, client or employee gifts, year end or Christmas bonuses. Available from the box office in denominations of £5.

The Theatre Club and Mailing List
Why not join our Theatre Club, 'The Ancient Order of Hippos'? Benefits include discounts on seats, car parking and taxis and priority booking for all events. Alternatively, there is the 'Keep in Touch' mailing list simply informing you of all events at the theatre. Leaflets for both are available in the theatre foyer.

Hippodrome Theatre Development Trust
Many of the amenities you now enjoy at the Hippodrome have been provided with the assistance of the Development Trust. Your support for the work of the Trust would be appreciated and details may be obtained from the Development Executive John Pearce at the Hippodrome Offices, phone 021-692-1363.

Smoking is not permitted in the auditorium. The use of cameras and tape recorders in this theatre is forbidden.

In accordance with the regulations of Birmingham City Council 1. The public may leave at the end of the performance by all exit doors and such doors must at that time be open 2. All gangways, passageways and staircases must be kept entirely free from chairs or any other obstructions 3. Persons shall not in any circumstances be permitted to stand or sit in any of the gangways intersecting the seating or to sit in any of the other gangways. If standing be permitted in the gangways at the sides and rear of the seating it shall be strictly limited to the number indicated in those positions 4. The Safety curtain must be lowered and raised in the presence of each audience.

CITY ASSEMBLY ROOMS, Hurst Street.

These rooms were originally independent too, but became part of the Birmingham Hippodrome. They could be hired for private functions but their main function was Ballroom Dancing. Proprietor W. Bird. The premises consisted of two separate floors, ground and first floor. In the 1930's it became Tony's Ballroom, this closed in 1958. In 1959 the top floor became The Shamrock Club and had a separate entrance in Hurst Street. The ground floor is now part of the Tivoli Bar at the Hippodrome. This advertisement appeared in "Midland Amusements" in August 1913.

CHILDRENS THEATRE, Kyrle Hall, Sheep Street, Birmingham.

The theatre opened in November 1925, it was the first Childrens Theatre to be opened in this country. The first play was "Knave of Hearts". In December of this year they put on a Nativity Play entitled "The Mystery of the Nativity". It was organised by the Birmingham Boy's and Girl's Union who represented 68 clubs.

— —— —

GOSTA GREEN HALL, Gosta Green.

Formerly the Delicia Cinema, was purchased by the City of Birmingham in 1951, Festival of Britain Year, for £25,000 and converted into a theatre. It was short lived and the premises were used as a Boxing Venue, BBC T.V. Studio and an Art Centre. It is now run by the Aston University, which is in close proximity.

— —— —

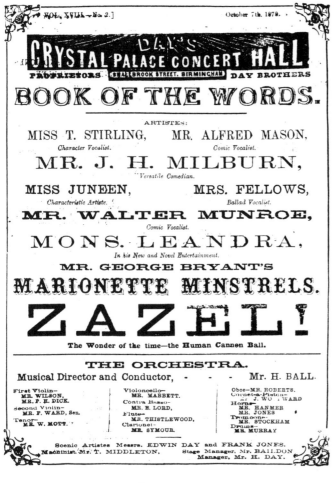

DAY'S PALACE OF VARIETIES

October 1885.

DAY'S CRYSTAL PALACE OF VARIETIES.

The proprietors of this excellently-conducted temple of amusement have every reason to be proud of the success that has attended their endeavours to please their patrons. This week there is another grand combination of talent, each item of the long and varied programme meeting with general approval. The bright particular stars of the week are Miss Eunice and the great Vance. Miss Vance, who has made her first appearance at this hall, has given one of the most charming entertainments we have listened to for some time. A most charming appearance, an expressive manner of singing, with a good compass, and a pleasing quality of voice, this lady is destined to become a great favourite. It is almost unnecessary to speak of Mr. Vance's qualifications (who is engaged for six nights only). This artist has reached a platform where he may be considered almost above criticism; so we content ourselves. He is still as great and deserving a favourite as ever, and he has met with an enthusiastic reception from his numerous admirers. Mdlle. Zara, from the Alhambra, London, has been one of the stars of the week. This lady is an excellent sentimental singer, with a good voice and style, and found that ready appreciation which her talented business so thoroughly deserved.

The Malaros give an excellent and refined drawing-room musical entertainment, and has been well received.

The American artistes, the Maxwells, in an original variety entertainment, entitled "A Summer Vacation," have been immensely successful, while the same may be said of Messrs. Rice, Melrose, and Lovell, whose successful negro entertainment has caused great merriment and enthusiastic recall.

Mr. Richard Schofield and Little Clemolo, with his dogs and monkeys, complete an unusually strong company. Mr. G. H. Macdermott is engaged for next week, who will be sure of an enthusiastic reception from his "legion" of friends. We are also given to understand the "Pinnauds," who made a "decided hit" during their last engagement, will shortly appear.

On dit.—That Paul Martinetti and his renowned clever ballet troupe, will appear at Day's during the ensuing season. It is quite superfluous to say they will meet with a most hearty reception·

This article was published in the Birmingham Dramatic News dated Saturday October 10th 1885.

THE EMPIRE THEATRE, 75, Smallbrook Street, corner of Hurst Street.

The theatre opened on Monday May 7th 1894 as the New Empire Palace of Varieties.   Proprietors, The Birmingham Empire Palace Ltd., it was advertised as 'The Most Beautiful Variety Theatre in England'.   It had an excellent Company of High Class Artists, George Chirgwin, Lucy Clarke, Ben Nathan, Gus Elen, Fred Milles, Two Macs, etc.   The Empire Grand Orchestra of thirty instrumentalists under the direction of Arthur Grimmett.   Prices of admission, Private Boxes £1.10s.6d. and £1.15s.0. Dress Circle 3s.,   Pit 1s.,   Gallery 6d.   Doors   opened at 7.00 pm show commenced at 7.30 pm. Managing Director Mr. H.W. Moss, General Manager Mr. Frank Allen, Acting Manager Mr. John Shaw.

Originally this was the site of the White Swan Public House.   This was taken over by James Day, he built a large hall on part of this Public House and installed a large crystal ball and mirrors and it became known as, Days Crystal Palace Concert Hall.   This opened on the 18th October 1862.   It was a very popular venue showing a diversity of entertainment.   It closed   in September 1893.   It was then sold to Moss Empires and closed and completely rebuilt at a cost of £18,000.   Architect Frank Matcham.   It then opened, as stated above, as the Empire Theatre.

Mr. A.W. Matcham was manager period 1894 to 1911 when he was presented with a testimonial as a mark of esteem.   In the 1920's Henry Raymond was the Resident Manager, a very popular character. The Musical Director was Edward da Costa.   It gave twice nightly performances, 6.40 and 8.50 pm. The theatre was destroyed in an enemy air raid on the city in 1941.   The building was demolished 10 years later as depicted in the above photograph.

30

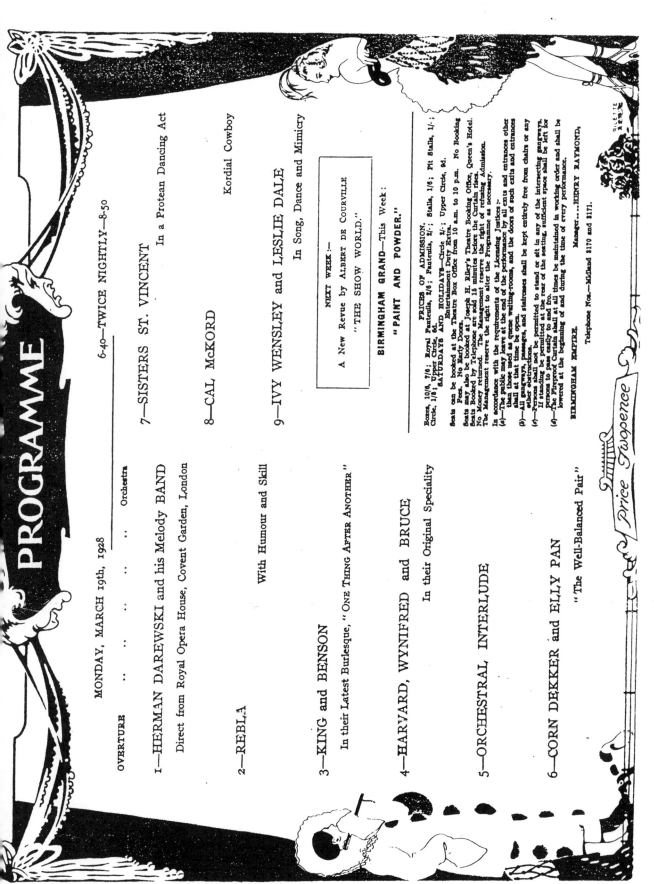

PROGRAMME

MONDAY, MARCH 19th, 1928

6·40—TWICE NIGHTLY—8·50

OVERTURE   ..   ..   Orchestra

1—HERMAN DAREWSKI and his Melody BAND

Direct from Royal Opera House, Covent Garden, London

2—REBLA

With Humour and Skill

3—KING and BENSON

In their Latest Burlesque, "ONE THING AFTER ANOTHER"

4—HARVARD, WYNIFRED and BRUCE

In their Original Speciality

5—ORCHESTRAL INTERLUDE

6—CORN DEKKER and ELLY PAN

"The Well-Balanced Pair"

7—SISTERS ST. VINCENT

In a Protean Dancing Act

8—CAL McKORD

Kordial Cowboy

9—IVY WENSLEY and LESLIE DALE

In Song, Dance and Mimicry

NEXT WEEK :—

A New Revue by ALBERT DE COURVILLE

"THE SHOW WORLD."

BIRMINGHAM GRAND—This Week :

"PAINT AND POWDER."

PRICES OF ADMISSION.

Boxes, 10/6, 7/6; Royal Fauteuils, 2/6; Fauteuils, 2/-; Stalls, 1/6; Pit Stalls, 1/-; Circle, 1/6; Upper Circle, 6d. Entertainment Duty Extra.

SATURDAYS AND HOLIDAYS—Circle 2/-; Upper Circle, 9d.

Seats can be booked at the Theatre Box Office from 10 a.m. to 10 p.m. No Booking Fees. No Early Doors.

Seats may also be booked at Joseph H. Riley's Theatre Booking Office, Queen's Hotel. Seats Booked by Telephone are sold 15 minutes before the Curtain rises. No Money returned. The Management reserve the right of refusing Admission. The Management reserve the right to alter the Programme as necessary.

In accordance with the requirements of the Licensing Justices :—

(a)—The public may leave at the end of the performance by all exits and entrances other than those used as gangways, waiting-rooms, and the doors of such exits and entrances shall at that time be open.

(2)—All gangways, passages, and staircases shall be kept entirely free from chairs or any other obstruction.

(3)—Persons shall not be permitted to stand or sit in any of the intersecting gangways. If standing be permitted at the rear of the seating, sufficient space shall be left for persons to pass easily to and fro.

(4)—The Fireproof Curtain shall at all times be maintained in working order and shall be lowered at the beginning of and during the time of every performance.

BIRMINGHAM EMPIRE.   Manager...HENRY RAYMOND,

Telephone Nos.—Midland 2170 and 2171.

Price Twopence

Birmingham Empire Program.

31

GRAND THEATRE, Corporation Street (next door to the King's Hall).

This theatre opened on the 14th of November 1883 with the showing of a special programme comprising of "Ici on parle Francais", "Good as Gold" and a musical, "At the Seaside". It had a seating capacity of 2,200 and had two circles, gallery, ground floor and 8 boxes. It was intended to call it 'New Theatre' but it was changed to 'Grand Theatre' before the opening date. The theatre was owned and managed by Andrew Melville. In 1907 it was purchased by Moss Empires, the interior was redesigned at a cost of £20,000, it was then known as the "Grand Theatre of Varieties", prices of admission 3d in the gallery to 2/−, boxes 5/− and 10/− each. It continued until 1930 when, on the 1st September it opened as a cinema, proprietors Universal Pictures Ltd., the film selected was "All Quiet on the Western Front" with Louis Wolheim and Lew Ayres. This was an epic film. It was only open as a cinema for a few years, closing on the 13th of May 1933. It was empty for a few years and then opened as "The Grand Casino Ballroom", (Mecca Dancing) it closed in 1960.

Grand Theatre, Birmingham.

SUMMER DRAMATIC SEASON !

WEEK COMMENCING MONDAY, MAY 21ST, 1906,

Special Production of the Emotional Play,

"EAST LYNNE" preceded by "HIS BAD ANGEL."

The Cast also includes :—Mr. Arthur Soames, Mr. E. Vanderlip, Mr. Harvey Long, Mr. Henry Bute, Mr. D. Dane, Mr. S. Appleby, Miss Annie Hill, Miss Launa Laurence, Miss Irene Rooke, and Miss Millie Edwin.

The New Grand Theatre.
CORPORATION STREET, BIRMINGHAM.

LAST TWO NIGHTS OF THE PANTOMIME,
"THE FORTY THIEVES,"
SPECIAL ATTRACTIONS.

Monday, Feb. 20, for a short season.
MR. J. W. TURNER'S GRAND ENGLISH
OPERA COMPANY.

Powerful Company, Full Band and Chorus.
Monday—"Fra Diavolo."
Tuesday—"Rohemian Girl."
Wednesday—"Faust."
Thursday morning—"Bohemian Girl."
Thursday evening—"Maritana."
Friday—"Marriage of Figaro."
Saturday morning—"Maritana."
Saturday evening—"Faust."

February 1888.

GRAND THEATRE,

CORPORATION STREET, BIRMINGHAM.

Sole Proprietor	Mr. J. W. TURNER
General Manager	Mr. VICTOR TURNER

SHAKESPEARIAN REVIVAL, 1906

Romeo and Juliet.

A Production of Unparalleled Magnificence.

Altogether the production will employ **100 Artistes**, and will be on such a magnificient scale that it will eclipse in beauty any presentation of the story hitherto seen.

Full & Powerful Chorus.   Augmented Orchestra.

MAGNIFICENT DRESSES, SCENERY AND ARMOUR.

Box Office 11 to 3.   Telephone 267.

February 1906.

Grand Theatre.

Proprietor   ...   .   A. MELVILLE.

Unprecedented Attraction.—TO-NIGHT, and During the Week, at 7.30, Grand Production, for the First Time on any stage, of an entirely New Comic Opera, entitled,

"ERMINIE."

Libretto by CLAXON BELLAMY and HARRY PAULTON ; Music by EDWARD JAKOBOWSKI.

Characters by Miss Florence St. John, Miss Melnotte, Miss M. A. Victor, Miss Kate Everleigh, Miss Edith Vane, and Miss Kate Munroe ; Mr. Harry Paulton, Mr. Frank Wyatt, Mr. Percy Compton, Mr. Horace Bolini, Mr. Fred Mervin, Mr. J. W. Bradbury, Mr. George Marler, and Mr. Henry Bracy ; assisted by a Company, Chorus, and Orchestra of about

ONE HUNDRED AND TEN PERFORMERS.

Powerful Chorus and Increased Orchestra, under the direction of Mr. A. Van Biene.

Business Manager (for "Erminie" Company), Mr. GILBERT TAIT.

Box Office now open daily, at the Theatre, from 11 till 3. Open at 7 ; early door at 6.30. Commence at 7.30. Second Price at 9.

SPECIAL NOTICE. — Notwithstanding the enormous expense attending this extraordinary engagement, there will be No Advance in the Usual Prices.

October 1885.

GRAND THEATRE,

CORPORATION STREET, BIRMINGHAM.

Sole Proprietor	Mr. J. W. TURNER
General Manager	Mr. VICTOR TURNER

MONDAY. FEBRUARY 5th, 1906,
FOR SIX NIGHTS,
Special Matinee, Thursday, Feb. 8, at 2.

IMPORTANT ENGAGEMENT OF

Mr. Cyril Maude's London Co.

IN

BEAUTY AND THE BARGE

By W. W. Jacobs and Louis N. Parker.

Preceded by

"THAT BRUTE SIMMONS,"

By Arthur Morrison and Herbert C. Sargent.

Box Office 11 to 3.   Telephone 267.

February 1906.

Grand Theatre.

Every Evening at 7-30,

THE DANITES.

MONDAY NEXT, "HOW THE POOR LIVE."

February 1888.

GRAND THEATRE,

CORPORATION STREET, BIRMINGHAM.

Sole Proprietor	Mr. J. W. TURNER
General Manager	Mr. VICTOR TURNER

Monday, April 9th.   1906

Balfe's Opera, in Four Acts,

SATANELLA

Count Rupert	Mr. J. W. Turner.
Arimanes	Mr. Sidney Clifford.
Brocacio	Mr. George Ridding.
Hortensio	Mr. Richard Cummings.
Karl	Mr. Charles Le Sueur.
Vizer	Mr. Sydney Appleby.
Lelia	Miss Constance Bellamy.
Stella	Miss Jessie Dennis.
Bertha	Miss Maud Esdale.
Satanella	Miss Kitty Brownless.

Tuesday, April 10th.

Verdi's Tragic Opera in Four Acts,

IL TRAVATORE

Manrico	Mr. F. J. Hargrave
Count Di Luna	Mr Harry Thornton
Ferrando	Mr. G. H. Ridding.
Ruiz	Mr. Newton.
Azucena	Miss Beatrice Hill.
Inez	Miss Ethel Locker.
Leonara	Miss Alice Boaden.

Wednesday, April 11th.

Bizet's Opera, in Four Acts,

CARMEN.

Don Jose, a Brigadier	Mr. J. W. Turner.
Escamillo, a Bullfighter	Mr. John Ridding.
Zunigar, an Officer	Mr. Frank Clark.
Morales, an Officer	Mr. William Anderson.
Dancalro | Smugglers |	Mr Geo. H Ridding.
Rememdado |	Mr. R. Cummings.
Lillas Pasta, an Innkeeper	Mr. Jessop
Michaola, a Peasant Girl	Miss Alice Boaden.
Frasquita | Gipsies |	Miss Stock.
Mercedes |	Miss Jessie Dennis.
AND	
Carmen	Miss Marie Burnett.

Dragoons, Cigar Girls. Gipsies. Smugglers, People, &c.

Thursday, April 12th.

Donnizetti's Opera, in three Acts,

DAUGHTER OF THE REGIMENT

Tonio	Mr. Charles Le Sueur.
Sergeant Sulpice	Mr. Sidney Clifford.
Hortensio	Mr. Richard Cummings.
Corporal	Mr George Ridding.
Countess	Miss Winifred Knightley.
Suzette	Miss Maud Esdale.
Marie	Miss Kitty Brownless.

Good Friday, April 13th.

SACRED CONCERT

By **Mr. J. W. TURNER and Principal members of his Opera Company.**

Saturday, April 14th.

Benedict's Charming Opera, in Three Acts, the

THE LILY OF KILLARNEY

Miles-na Coppaline	Mr. F. J. Hargrave.
Hardress Cregan	Mr. Chas. Le Sueur.
Danny Mann	Mr. Tom Griffiths.
Father Tom	Mr. William Anderson
Corrigan	Mr. George Ridding.
Mrs Cregan	Miss Marie Burnett
Annie Chute	Miss Ethel Locker.
Sheela	Miss Maud Esdale.
Eily	Miss Kitty Brownless.

KING'S HALL (Late Old Central Hall)

Next door to the Grand Theatre in Corporation Street. Proprietors and managers J.P. Moore and B. Kennedy. It opened in September 1907 showing Vaudeville Entertainment, the acts included Miss Mollie Revell, The Lady Baritone and Song Illustrator, Mr. Clarence Turner, The Quaint Lancashire Humorist, in Song and Patter, Mons. Otto Ethardo, The Continental Juggler. This was followed by Ediscope and Barnum's Electric Pictures. It gave three performances daily 3 p.m., 7 p.m., and 9 p.m. Prices of admission Circle 1/- Early Door 1/3; Side Boxes 6d; Early Door 8d; Pit Stalls 4d; Early Door 6d; Pit 2d; Early Door 3d. Children half-price to Circle and Boxes only. On Saturday December 7th they

put on a benefit matinee when the entire proceeds were donated to the 'Birmingham Mail Christmas Tree Fund'. By 1911 it ceased variety shows and operated as a cinema. It finally closed c. 1932.

TEMPERANCE HALL, Temple Street, Birmingham.

Opened in 1858 built at a cost of £3,298 was the H.Q. of the Temperance Society. The building had a ground floor with a stage and the first floor had a gallery running round three sides. It had a seating capacity of 900. It was re-built in 1901. It was licensed for singing, dancing, music and cinematograph performances. It was let to various organisations for entertainment shows. Orchestral concerts were a regular feature. It was the venue for Billy Mander's Quauntesques. In July 1910 it showed Kinemacolor Animated Pictures. It showed normal films in 1921 under the management of J.H. Lear Hall. It closed c. 1932.

The Quaintesques.

THE LONDON MUSEUM and CONCERT HALL, 143 Digbeth.

Opened on the 24th of December 1863. Proprietor George Biber. In 1880 the General Manager was E.G. Goldsmith. In 1885 it was taken over by Donald McInnes and under the management of Robert Hall. In 1888 the proprietor was Alex Macgregor and in 1890 changed its name to Canterbury Tavern and Music Hall. In 1894 it was taken over by Alfred Hardy who changed the name, once again, to Pavilion Tavern and Music Hall. In 1892 Robert Hall took it over. In 1896 Harry Ashmore took over and he reverted it back to its original name London Museum and Concert Hall. In 1896 William Coutts took over and called it Coutts' Theatre. This flourished for about 2 years presenting some of the popular plays of the day, 'Trilby', 'Dr. Jekylle and Mr. Hyde', 'Uncle Tom's Cabin' and 'Sweetheart' to name but a few. George A. Parker was the leading man and producer. Mrs. Parker (Annie Thursfield) was his leading lady. On Sundays Lantern Services were held in connection with Mr. Pentland's Street Robins Movement. Numerous outings were arranged for poor children to be taken on trips to the country during the summer months. It closed in 1900. In 1912 it opened as The Bull Ring Cinema. The building was originally on the corner of Park Street and Digbeth but in 1897 The Royal George Public House was built in front of it. It's address then had to be altered to No. 2, Park Street. The building is still there today.

THE LONDON MUSEUM CONCERT HALL.

Messrs. Ellier and Alza, described as the "Flying Comets," head the list of attractions here. The "Comets" are certainly stars of great magnitude, and as they do their business in the air they have not chosen a bad *nom de plume*. Their performance is remarkable for the ease in which they go through it, but to the uninitiated eye it seems dangerous, and we heard several of the audience express their opinions as to the advisability of a net, one gentleman (?) being somewhat alarmed for the safety of his spouse, remarking, "Come on, Missis ! let's do a shift to the side—its dangerous to be safe down here." However, there is not much to fear, as Messrs. Ellier and Alza are too well practised to make much of a mistake. Miss Amy Height, who looks black at everybody, sings remarkably well. As some individuals may misunderstand the last sentence it may be as well to state that the cause of this lady's black looks is her dusky complexion, for she is what is described on the stage as "a cullud gal," and a good-looking one, too. Mr. Sam Stream, an old favourite in the town, still pleases with his flowing melodies and comic impersonations. His characters are well made up, and his business throughout is full of humour. The Sisters Le Blanche, a charming trio, sing, dance, and act in a highly creditable manner, and the veteran comedian and dancer, Teddy Mosedale, is as good and sprightly as ever, and equally as big a favourite as he was when he fulfilled his first starring engagement here, tw——, well, many years ago. "Teddy" is a good old comic of the good old school, who gained their reputation by making people laugh, instead of cadging applause by singing political humbug, as many self-styled stars have done of late years.

Thursday next is set apart for the annual benefit of Mr. McInnes. on which occasion a number of extra attractions will be provided in addition to the company engaged. We trust he will receive a bumper.

December 1885.

London Museum.

Proprietor ... ... D. McINNES.

GREAT ATTRACTION.

First appearance of those great Gymnasts, the FLYING COMETS.
AMY HEIGHT, THE THREE GRACES,
SAM STREAM, MISS LE BLANCH.
Great Success.
Last six nights of SISTERS LE BLANC, TEDDY MOSEDALE,
"THE BASHER KING ; and Grand Star Company.

Manager, R. HALL.

THE PIGEON CHARMER
LONDON MUSEUM.

THE NEW STAR THEATRE of VARIETIES, Snow Hill. Opened on the 23rd of November 1885. Mr. W.R. Inshaw was the enterprising proprieter and a son of the well known proprieter of the Steam Clock Hall in Ladywood. The manager was Mr. E.A. Creswell. The principal performers being the Leglere Troupe of marvellous acrobats, Messrs Henderson and Stanley, The Living Marionettes, Leoni Clarke and his Pigeons, Tyroleum, Florrie Gallimore extemporaneous, Charley Harrison and those great local favourites, The Creswell Trio who introduced in their sketch one of Frank James's Canine Wonders. It cost £15,000 to build but only lasted 12 months. After substantial alterations and additions it re-opened on Boxing Day in December 1886 and re-named Queen's Theatre and Opera House. The Gala performance was attended by Joseph Chamberlain for the showing of the Bohemian Girl. In the early 1900's it changed it's name to The Metropole Theatre under the management of Walter Melville. It showed full blooded melodrama, such as Monty Cristo, The Dangers of London, The Grip of Iron and The Red Barn. In March 1908 a special production of The Streets of Birmingham was performed. The Theatre had a seating capacity, at this time of Gallery 700, Circle 350, Ground Floor 530. It closed in 1911 and later opened as a cinema.

STAR THEATRE OF VARIETIES
"SNOW HILL"
OPEN EVERY NIGHT, AT 7-30

THE IMPERIAL THEATRE, corner of Clyde Street and High Street, Bordesley.

Opened on the 2nd October 1899 at a cost of £25,000 with the showing of the play, "Sporting Life" a drama by Cecil Raleigh and Seymour Hicks. Proprietors Chas. E. Machin and James Bacon. In 1903 it was taken over by Moss Empires Ltd., and refurbished at a cost of £6,000. It then changed its name to BORDESLEY Palace. Prices of admission 3d, 6d and 1/—. Seats in Private Boxes 1/6. It was advertised as showing High Class Music and Varieties. W. Goodwin was acting manager in 1910. In 1913 it was leased to Powell's Playhouse Limited under the management of Mr. H.E. Cox. It closed in 1929 and the final performance was the showing of the famous melodrama, "Maria Marten" or "The Murder in the Red Barn." It had a seating capacity of 1,296. It then opened as a cinema. During the Second World War the building was requisitioned by the Ministry of Food and used as a food store. The building was demolished in 1957.

It would be difficult to single out a more sprightly, cheerful and hard working singing artiste than Miss Marie Loftus who topped the bill week commencing June 25th 1906. Since her debut at Leeds, when she drew twenty five shilling a week, she has appeared at all the principal halls in England, America and South Africa. Also appearing on the bill were the famous Delevines in their New Musical Melange, "Flipp and Floop". and also New Macs, J.P. Ling, The Dorrels and the Corri Dereve's Company in "Heart Strings".

BORDESLEY PALACE,
THEATRE AND STAGE CIRCUS OF VARIETIES,
OPPOSITE BORDESLEY STATION.

Proprietary-Moss' Empires Ltd. Chairman—H. Edward Moss.
Managing Director—Oswald Stoll. Assistant Director and Chief of Staff—Frank Allen. District Manager—H. Wharton.
Acting Manager—Edward Foster.

MONDAY, MAY 21st, 1906, and twice nightly during the week at 6.15 and 8.40.

THE FAMOUS CRAGGS
'BILLY'
THE NEW STEWARD OF THE "CHANNEL QUEEN."
A Sketch Full of Comedy and Skill.

George Tacius   Marie Collins   Herbert Shelley
Kitts & Windrum   The Jagos
The Wig Chase on the American Bioscope

THE MARLO & DUNHAM TRIO
who seem to have reached finality in Feats on the Horizontal Bar

Prices:—Private Boxes 5/- for 4 persons, Orchestra Stalls 1/-
Grand Circle 6d., Pit 4d., Gallery Mondays, Saturdays and Bank Holidays, 3d., Tuesdays, Wednesdays, Thursdays and Fridays 2d.

Miss Dolly Eldworthy's Company appeared week commencing July 16th 1906 in an Episode in the Life of King Charles II (period 1600) entitled "The Orange Girl" a drama by H. Leslie and Nicholas Rowe. Also appearing on the bill were Belloni's Cockatoos, a marvellous example of bird training.

ASTON THEATRE ROYAL, Aston Road North, Aston.
On the 23rd September 1892 an agreement was signed between George and Robert Hall to erect a theatre on this site. This was duly built and opened the following year at a cost of £6,500. It had financial problems and in 1894 was sold to Charles Barnard who made extensive alterations. The General Manager was E. Hewitson, Acting Manager F. Whittles. It was further refurbished in 1912 at a cost of £7,000. It had a seating capacity of 2,000. It closed in 1926 and on the 12th December 1927 opened as The Astoria Cinema. This closed on the 26th November 1955 and was converted into a T.V. Studio.

ASTON ROYAL.

Sole Lessee ...	Mr. Chas. BARNARD.
General Manager ...	Mr. E. HEWITSON.
Acting Manager ...	Mr. F. WHITTLES.

MONDAY, OCT. 1st, 1906, & every evening during the week.

FREDK. MELVILLE'S Co.

in the famous and popular drama—

Between Two Women

By Frederick Melville.

Special Supplement to the "BIRMINGHAM PROGRAMME OF AMUSEMENTS."

ASTON THEATRE ROYAL.

Proprietor ... MR. CHAS. BARNARD. General Manager ... MR. E. HEWITSON. Acting Manager ... MR. F. WHITTLES

Monday, January 20, 1908,

For Six Nights and One Matinee.

Matinee, Saturday, January 25th. *Reduced Prices for Children to all Parts.*

MESSRS. DOTTRIDGE & LONGDEN'S Grand Comic Christmas Pantomime:

"ROBINSON ...

.. CRUSOE."

Written, arranged, and produced by Mr. H. FLOCKTON FOSTER.

Under the Direction of ERNEST DOTTRIDGE.

☞ SMOKING PERMITTED IN ALL PARTS.

PRICES OF ADMISSION:

Ordinary Doors at 7. Private Boxes to hold Six, 10 6. Single Box Seats, 2 -. Stalls, 1 6. Circle, 1 -. Pit, 6d. Gallery, 4d.
Early Doors at 6.30. Stalls, 1 9. Circle, 1 3. Pit, 9d. Gallery, 6d
HALF PRICE AT NINE O'CLOCK TO ALL PARTS (Gallery excepted). Boxes, 10 6. Single Seats, 2 -. Stalls, 1 9. Circle, 1 3.
Box Plans now open at the Theatre between 10 a.m and 4 p.m. each day.
All communications to be addressed to MR. F. WHITTLES.

⇒ NEW THEATRE ROYAL, ⇐

ASTON CROSS.

Proprietor and Manager ... ... Mr. ROBERT HALL.

GRAND OPENING NIGHT, MONDAY, AUGUST 7th, 1893, BANK HOLIDAY,

UNDER THE DISTINGUISHED PATRONAGE AND PRESENCE OF

Capt. GRICE-HUTCHINSON, M.P., and Magistrates.

The New Theatre has been Built on Plans from that Eminent Architect, Mr. W. H. WARD, Paradise Street, by Mr. WILLIAM BLOOR, of Alma Street, Aston. The splendid New Scenery by Messrs. W. S. TODD, DOWNING, BOSWORTH, and Assistants. The Stage with all the latest improvements has been laid by Messrs. T. J. WOOD, NORTHCOTE, and Assistants. The Magnificent Stage Front by Messrs. DE JONG & Co., Camden Works, Camden Town, London. The Gas Arrangements on Stage by TOLLERTON, of Leeds; in front by Messrs. FLETCHER & SON, New John Street. The Furnishing, Curtains, &c., by that pre-eminent Firm, A. R. DEAN, Corporation Street, Birmingham.

Great Engagement of

MARTIN ADESON AND WALTER SUMMERS' BURLESQUE COMPANY

is an Entirely New and Original Three-Act Burlesque,

NAUGHTY TITANIA, or, a Mortal's Adventures in Fairy Land.

New and Original Music composed by JULIEN B. WILSON, Esq., R.A.M.

CAPTIVATING DANCES. CHARMING SCENERY. A HOST OF PRETTY WOMEN, including the Celebrated

VENUS BALLET TROUPE

First-Class Company of celebrated Artistes.

MISS DOLLY VERDON
Principal Boy, H. DUNDAS, Esq's, Pantodome.

MR. CHARLES ADESON
Principal Comedian, Princess's Theatre, Glasgow, Pantomime.

MR. ARTHUR VERNE
Comedian, Princess's Theatre Pantomime.

MARTIN ADESON
Principal Comedian, Shakespeare Theatre, Liverpool, Pantomime.

WALTER SUMMERS
Principal Comedian, Princess's Theatre, Bristol, Pantomime.

Specialities introduced into the Fancy Fair Scene:—M. GALVERTO, Shot-arm-worker and Mimic. DROFLA, the Renowned Juggler. Miss LIZZIE PAYNE, Expert Dancer.

First Production on any Stage of

NAUGHTY TITANIA

BY STANLEY ROGERS, ESQ.

MORTALS.

Duke De Oofless	...	... Mr. PAUL RUSSELL
Madge	(his Daughter)	... Miss POLLIE BLAKE
Agamemnon Fitz Nobody	...	Mr. ARTHUR VERNE
Robert Peeler	(of the Guards)	Miss NORAH CARONNE
Cavalier De High Jenks	(of the Force)	... Miss MARIAN VYNER
Socrates Smith		Mr. MARTIN ADESON
Jemima, his Wife		Mr. WALTER SUMMERS
Sir Washington Spoon	} a couple of { Trippers	... Miss FAY AXTEN
Hon. Simpleton Shirt Front		Miss MAUD HINCHLIFFE
Angela		Miss LILA DOYLE
Malvina		Miss JULIA HINCHLIFFE

IMMORTALS.

Oberon	(King of the Fairies)	... Miss DOLLY VERDON
Titania	(Queen of the Fairies)	Miss MAY HETHERINGTON
Puck	(their Page)	Mr. CHARLES ADESON
Morpheus		Miss CLARA ARNOLD
Gauze Wing		Miss AMY ALLAN
Glow Worm	} Fairies {	Miss MAY WILD
Butterfly		Miss CORA GREY
May Bloom		Miss DORA VESEY

ACT 1.—ISLE OF MAN   W. S. TODD.   **ACT 2.—FANCY FAIR**   W. S. TODD.
ACT 3.   **FAIRYLAND**   W. S. TODD.

PRODUCED UNDER THE DIRECTION OF MR. WALTER SUMMERS.

Business Manager ... Mr. MARTIN ADESON   Musical Conductor ... JULIEN WILSON R.A.M.
Stage Manager ... Mr. WALTER SUMMERS   Wardrobe Mistress ... Mrs. FORRESTER

Complete Installation of ELECTRIC LIGHT by Messrs. HEMMING & Co., Limited, 55, Snow Hill, Birmingham.

PRICES OF ADMISSION:—
ORCHESTRA STALLS, 2s.   STALLS, 1s.6d.   PIT (Cushioned), 1s.   AMPHITHEATRE STALLS, 9d.   GALLERY, 6d.
Doors open at 7 o'clock, commence at 7.30 prompt.

Resident Musical Conductor, Mr. WALTER DENTON.   Resident Scenic Artist, Mr. W. S. TODD.   Resident Master Carpenter, Mr. T. J. WOOD.

ASTON HIPPODROME, Potter's Lane, (off High Street) Aston.

Grand Opening Performance was on Monday December 7th 1908, (see display notice). Director of Entertainment — Fred Wilmot. Manager — T.H. Middleton. It was built at a cost of £10,000. Architects James Lister & Co. 1912–1935 the manager was Tommy Willis, he was superseded by Tommy Fitzgibbon. On the 12th February 1938 the theatre was burned down and it was closed for 6 months. It was fully restored at a cost of £30,000. In 1942 the manageress was Mrs. M. Hudson and in 1946 the Resident Manager was Maurice Zand. In 1951 it was under the direction of F.J. Butterworth. Manager and Licensee Fredk. J. Studd. It then gave performances twice daily — 2.30 p.m. and 7.15 p.m. Prices of Admission Boxes 24/– Orchestra Stalls and Dress Circle 6/–., Royal Circle and Centre Stalls 5/–, Pit Stalls and Back Circle 3/6, Balcony 1/6. In 1960 the proprietors were F.J. B. Theatres Ltd., under the management of J. Tomkinson. It closed on 4th June 1960, the final performance being a revue called, 'The A–Z in Striptease'. It later opened as a Bingo Hall, the building was finally demolished September 1980. Over the years well known 'stars' have appeared. Wee Georgie Wood, George Formby, Gracie Fields, Sid Fields, Ted Ray, Sandy Powell, Morecambe and Wise, and Larry Grayson.

THE NEW MINOR THEATRE, Allison Street, Digbeth.

One of the long forgotten theatres in Birmingham, it was only open for a few years. The two playbills cover the period 1835 to 1838. It closed 1838.

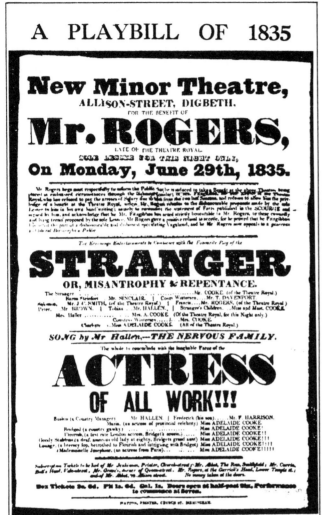

This playbill dated June 29th 1835 advertising a transitory and long forgotten theatre in this City. It announces a benefit for a Mr. Rogers, an actor from the Theatre Royal in New Street, who was in "embarrassed" circumstances because, he claimed, Mr. Fitzgibbon, the sole lessee at that time, had not paid him his salary for two seasons and had refused him a benefit at the Theatre Royal. It would appear that Mr. Rogers had written certain statements in a publication called "The Scourge", and on being invited to contradict them he refused, having (to his own satisfaction) "proved that Fitzgibbon had acted the part of a dishonourable and dishonest speculating Vagabond."

BIRMINGHAM REPERTORY THEATRE

in association with

DUNCAN C WELDON
with PAUL GREGG & LIONEL BECKER
in association with JEROME MINSKOFF

14 May - 19 June 1984

REX HARRISON   CLAUDETTE COLBERT

NICOLA PAGETT

MICHAEL GOUGH   MADGE RYAN

and

FRANCIS MATTHEWS

in

AREN'T WE ALL

by FREDERICK LONSDALE

with

ANNIE LAMBERT

ROBERT GLADWELL   JOHN INGRAM
BEN BAZELL   TIMOTHY PETERS

and

JOHN PRICE

Directed by

CLIFFORD WILLIAMS

Sets by   Costumes by   Lighting by
FINLAY JAMES   JUDITH BLAND   MARK PRITCHARD

Rex Harrison.

Claudette Colbert.

BIRMINGHAM REPERTORY THEATRE
1984
18 June - 14 July
(Reduced Price Previews 15 and 16 June)

WORLD PREMIERE

SILVER LADY

by
Liane Aukin

The story of Ivy Benson and her All Girls Band and the struggles and trials of a woman pursuing with quiet determination a career in what was normally considered to be a male stronghold. The play spans the years before the Second World War up to the present day.

Directed by
PETER FARAGO

Sets by   Costumes by
GEOFFREY   DEIDRE
SCOTT   CLANCY

Lighting by
MICHAEL
ROWNTREE

1987

October 16th 1879.

GAIETY, 88, 89, 90, Coleshill Street.

Opened on the 24th June 1846 by Henry Holder who was the proprietor of the Rodney Inn at No.87. It was then known as Holders Hotel and Concert Hall. In 1863 the proprietors were Soward and Gardiner and in 1867 it was taken over by John Soward, Junior. In 1871 it was taken over by John Judd and Company who changed the name to The Birmingham Concert Hall. They continued as proprietors until 1876 when Phillips and Chowles took over. In 1886 Charles Barnard became the proprietor, he changed the name, to The Gaiety Concert Hall. In 1896 this was run by the Gaiety Trust and in 1897 was re-named The Gaiety Theatre of Varieties, this time run by the Birmingham Gaiety Theatres of Varieties Limited, the manager appointed was Albert Bushell. In 1910 P.D. Elbourne was appointed manager and in 1912 T. Allan Edwardes. When it closed in 1920 the proprietor and lessee was Ben. Kennedy. This was a very popular music hall of high esteem, having a seating capacity of 3,500. It had a fine organ played by Mr. Sola. In its early days patrons had to be properly dressed and wear top hats before allowed admission (see photograph). It closed in 1920 and the same year opened as a cinema. This closed on the 29th November 1969.

BIRMINGHAM CONCERT HALL.

We are pleased to see that the little unpleasantness referred to in our last issue has been amicably arranged in the manner we suggested, the happy result being to give general satisfaction to all concerned. This week's company is much the same as last, Mr. Fred. Cairns still being the principal attraction; although he has big rivals for public favour in Mr. Alf. Baker, and Miss Nellie Beresford, whose sketch, entitled "Night Duty," meets with well-merited applause. Two wonderfully clever gymnasts are Messrs. Voltyne and Horton, whose gyrations on the double bar are simply marvellous, and whose entertainment is not only startling but funny as well. The charming serio-comic, Miss Jessie Harte, continues to please with the pretty songs and dances. A bold bid for popularity is made by Mr. Fred. Percy, in his life-like delineation of an old negro, whose age and infirmities cannot hinder him from indulging in a taste of the sort of enjoyment he had "in the days when I was young." Mr. Percy thoroughly deserves the applause awarded him, for he is an artiste who studies every detail of his business, which but few in his line seem to bother about. The Sisters Lindon, the musical belles, are old and tried favourites, and it is needless to say that they meet with a large amount of success. Madlle. De Lonn gives a novel entertainment, concluding with balancing two ships of war, during what appears to be a heavy carronade. The Sisters Kent complete a good company.

This article was published in the Birmingham Dramatic News dated Saturday, October 10th. 1885.

10th October 1885.

BIRMINGHAM CONCERT HALL.

CURZON HALL, Corner of Suffolk Street and Holliday Street, Birmingham.

This large building was erected in 1864 as an exhibition hall and had seating for up to 3,000. The foundation stone was laid by Viscount George Nathaniel Curzon, English Statesman and Viceroy of India 1899–1905, whom the hall was named after. He was also the President of the National Dog Society and it was home and venue for their Annual National Dog Show. In February 1879 Newsome's Hippodrome and Circus put on a show, (see notice). In the Sept/Oct. period of the following year a play entitled "Temple of Japan" was presented, this included a cast of 30 male and female performers. In addition to this a variety performance was included including "Tommy the Wolf", horses and musical clowns. Prices of admission 6d to 2/6. Over the following years numerous forms of entertainment were shown including Minstrel Shows, Variety Concerts and in January 1907 The Royal Italian Circus having over 200 performing animals. 1899 was the commencement of the putting on of animated pictures by Waller Jeffs'. It later opened as a full time cinema known as the New Century Picture Theatre. During the first World War the building was used as a recruiting office. After extensive alterations it opened on 9th March 1925 as the West End Cinema and Ballroom.

CURZON HALL,
BIRMINGHAM.

Curzon Hall,
BIRMINGHAM.

To-night and every Evening at 8.
Matinees on Mondays, Thursdays and Saturdays at 2.30.
TELEPHONE 4373.

ENORMOUS AND CONTINUED SUCCESS OF

THE ROYAL
Italian Circus

The only Exhibition of its kind in the whole World.

As given Twice Recently by Royal Command before
their Majesties the
KING AND QUEEN
And Royal Family at Buckingham Palace.

Constant Change of Programme
OVER 200
PERFORMING ANIMALS.

☞ TRULY A SIGHT OF A LIFETIME ☜

Reserved Seats (Numbered) 2/6. Unreserved 2/-
and 1/6. Side Elevations 1/- Balcony 6d. Gallery 3d.
Children under 10 years half-price to all parts except
Gallery. Plan of Reserved Seats and Tickets at Messrs.
Harrison's Pianoforte Warehouse, Colmore Row.

Curzon Hall,
BIRMINGHAM.

Every Evening at 8, except Saturdays at 7-45.
MATINEES: MONDAYS, THURSDAYS, & SATURDAYS at 3

INSTANTANEOUS AND ENORMOUS SUCCESS OF
WILLIAM (the Only and Original)
HAMILTON'S
LATEST EXCURSIONS
FAR AND NEAR,
AND
Powerful Variety Company
OF STAR ARTISTES.

Prices: 3s. 2s. 1s. 6d.
Half-price at 9 o'clock to all parts except 6d. Seats.
Children Half-price, except 6d. Seats.
Early Doors at 7 o'clock, 3d. extra to all parts.
Ordinary Doors at 7-30.

BINGLEY HALL, King Edward's Place, (off Broad Street) Ladywood.

A popular venue for all types of popular entertainment and exhibition over its 133 years of existence. It opened in 1850. It was leased by a Mr. Tonks, in 1852, he had extensive interior alterations and fitted the hall out as an amphitheatre to seat over 4,000 patrons, he named it Tonks Colosseum. In 1854 he renamed it New Theatre and presented numerous popular plays including, 'The Merchant of Venice' the Shakespeare comedy. This only lasted a few years and the hall reverted to its original usage. Pat Collins put on his Christmas Circus show for a number of years. The British Theatre Exhibition was presented, period May 23 to June 18th 1949. Organised by the Birmingham Post in association with Sir Barry Jackson and the Arts Council of Great Britain.

This photograph was taken in April 1984 when the International Custom & Sports Car Show was on, this was one of the last exhibitions to be held there. The entire building was demolished shortly afterwards. The area is now part of the site for the new Civic Centre project.

STEAM CLOCK MUSIC HALL, 23 Morville Street (on the corner of Sherborne Street) Ladywood.

Opened in 1883 and was run in conjunction with the Steam Clock Tavern run by John Inshaw. It was a very popular local hall but primative in construction. It had a seating capacity of around 900. The proprietor, period 1884 to 1887 was Mr. W.R. Inshaw. Thomas Hall then took over until 1894 when Wm. Rudge became the proprietor. In 1895 it changed its name to The Ladywood Palace of Varieties, proprietor Mrs. Ellen Rudge, she was superseded the following year by H. Cruise. In 1902 the proprietor was Gus. Levaine. It closed in June 1910 and opened as the Ladywood Picture Palace showing Vaudeville and the latest Pictures. This closed in 1914 when the Ledsam Picture House was built, this was only about 250 yards away.

December 1885.

The Steam Clock,

MORVILLE STREET.

———

Proprietor ... ... Mr. W. R. INSHAW.

———

EVERY EVENING AT EIGHT.

———

GREAT SUCCESS OF

PROFESSOR EVANS

AND GRAND STAR COMPANY.

10th October 1885.

STEAM CLOCK MUSIC HALL

———

The company at this music hall calls for no special mention this week, although several new artistes have appeared, foremost of whom is Professor Evans, who, with his highly-trained dogs and monkeys, affords a vast amount of amusement. The everlasting Joe Maurice is still here, and in conjuction with Mr. Fred Lee, the facial contortionist, and Miss Maggie Rhodes, the clever child actress, an entertainment which suits the audience to a T is nightly given. Altogether, the evenings entertainment is good, and worthy of the popularity it meets with.

Comments published in the Birmingham Dramatic News on 10th October 1885.

NEW THEATRE ROYAL, Aston Road North, Aston.

On the 23rd September 1892 an agreement was signed between George and Robert Hall to erect a theatre on this site, this was duly built and opened on Bank Holiday Monday 7th August 1893. (See full details on copy programme). This closed in 1926 and on the 12th December 1927 opened as the ASTORIA CINEMA. Seating capacity 1,194. The films chosen were The British Legion Film, "Remembrance" with Capt. Rex. Davis M.C., Enid Stamp and Alf Goddard. The other film was, "The Fighting Stallion" with Yalima Canutt. This closed on 26th November 1955 with the showing of the film, "The Dambusters" with Michael Redgrave, Richard Todd, Basil Sydney and Patrick Barr playing the principle roles. After closure the premises were converted into a T.V. Studio, the first performance was screened on the 17th February 1956. In 1974 it was taken over by BRMB Radio Station.

The New ADELPHI THEATRE, rear of 66, Moor Street.

Opened c 1863, the sole Lessee and Manager was Mr. H.P. Grattan. Brilliant Chandeliers were erected to grace the interior of the building and adjacent ones had to be demolished to make way for the construction of Albert Street.

Moor Street was one of the main city centre streets at this time proceeding from the Bull Ring to Stafford Street. All that is left of it now is the entrance to Moor Street Station. It is now known as The Queensway and Moor Street, Queensway.

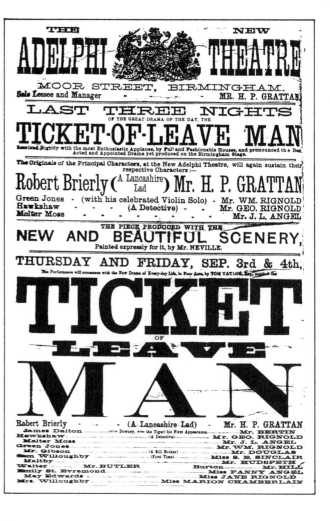

ROYAL CRECIAN AMPHITHEATRE, Moor Street.

A mystery theatre (or circus). No positive records in Birmingham Directories and no year shown on the above programme. It was in the mid 19th century, of that I am certain but, was it in a marquee on open ground, rented for the season? According to the Encyclopaedic Dictionary an amphitheatre is an oval or circular building with seats rising in tiers round an open arena.

The **UNIQUE THEATRE,** (late Weaman's Museum) Top of Temple Street, City Centre.

The actual date of opening is unknown but on May 22nd 1838 it held a farewell night for the benefit of Master G. Grossmith, who was then nearly 10 years of age, he appeared, assisted by his brother, in Three New Pieces, Part I, The March of Time, Part II, Next Door Neighbour, Part III, The Bell, The Bear and the Baker. Prices of admission Boxes 2/6. Pit 1/6. Gallery 1/-. Doors opened at a quarter before eight.

MASONIC HALL, 91-92 New Street, City centre.

Opened in 1875, in 1880 Dr. Bell Fletcher, J.P. was the Chairman.

It was a popular Concert Hall. Catlin's Royal Pierrots appeared there annually. Prices of admission 2/-, 1/6, 1/- and 6d.

In c 1908 it was re-named, Theatre de Luxe, Proprietors Electric Theatres (1908) Ltd., under the management of A. Fletcher, presenting the latest and best examples of cinematography. In November 1930 it opened as the Forum Cinema, this closed on the 9th April 1983.

CARLTON THEATRE, corner of Saltley Road and Nechells Place.

Opened on Monday, July 16th 1900. The sole owner and Manager being Mr. Arthur Carlton, Acting Manager, Mr. John Matthews, see full details on the programme copy, this was printed on silk and presented to all patrons as they entered the theatre. The theatre cost £14,000 and consisted of a large gallery, Pit stalls, dress circle and six boxes, Architect Thomas Guest. In 1906 the Acting Manager was Jas. Alexandra and the following year he took over control of the theatre. One of its attractions was an all Ladies String Orchestra. In 1911 it was re-named, Birmingham Coliseum and Gaiety, the General Manager was P.D. Elbourne. In 1921 it opened as a cinema and closed in the early 1940's.

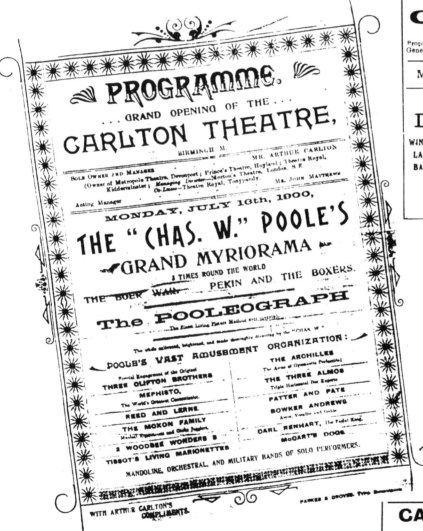

HOLTE THEATRE, Aston Lower Grounds, Aston.

A licence was granted and the theatre was opened in May 1879, closed in 1886. Managing director was Mr. H.G. Quilter. Stage manager Mr. Walter Raynham. The opening address was given by Mr. Raynham. The plays selected were:- Mr. Broughton's "Ruth's Romance" and "Light and Shade". The orchestra was directed by Seaton Ricks. Doors opened at 6.30. Curtain rises at 7.00 p.m. closed at 10.30 p.m. Prices of admission Reserved seats 2/-, Unreserved seats 1/-, Gallery sixpence. On Saturday March 6th 1880 Chas. Webb's popular drama "The Courier of Lyons" was shown.

The area was open for various types of entertainment including a Skating Rink and an Aquarium. You could purchase a season ticket to the grounds for One Guinea, this entitled you to admission to the Theatre which was in the Great Hall.

You could obtain transport, to the area by Omnibus or Train to Witton Station.

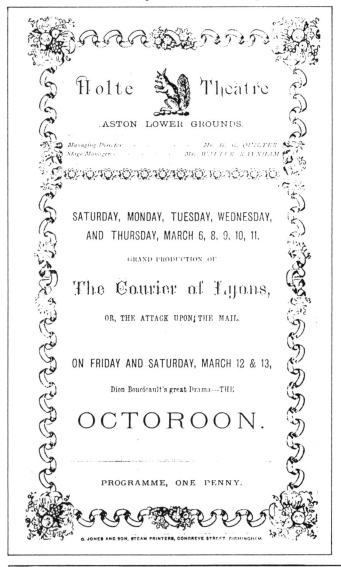

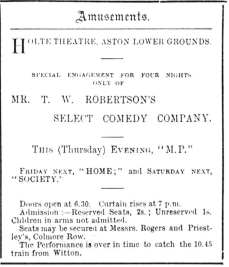

23rd October 1879.

17th April 1880.

The PALACE THEATRE, Summer Hill Road, Spring Hill, Birmingham.

Opened on the 19th December 1911 and was advertised as showing beautiful Motion Pictures, Illustrated song and Selected Variety. It gave twice nightly performances 6.45 and 9.00. Prices of admission 2d, 3d and 6d. Proprietors Moss Empires Limited.

In the 1930's it was taken over by the A.B.C. Circuit. It had a seating capacity of 861. It was demolished in 1981 and a new factory, Rabone Chesterman Ltd built on the site in 1984.

The NEWTOWN PALACE, New Town Row, Aston, Birmingham.

Opened on Monday 5th January 1914 advertising High Class Pictures and Selected Variety. It had accommodation for 2,000. Prices of admission 2d, 3d, 4d & 6d. Proprietors Moss Empires Limited. It was one of the popular cine-variety halls of the period. It had a full size stage and seven dressing rooms. It finally closed on 22nd April 1961, later opening as a Bingo and Social Club run by Ladbrookes Ltd., this closed in 1983. The building is still standing today but is derelict.

The ELITE PICTURE PALACE, situated on the corner of Bordesley Green and Crown Road, Bordesley Green.

Opened on the 9th of August 1913 advertised as showing General Variety and Pictures. Secretary was Chas. W. Cooke. It had a seating capacity of 1,327. Prices of admission 3d and 4d in the stalls and 6d in the Lounge. Music was provided by the Melford Trio and Dora Denmark. The films were preceded by variety acts or revues. The building was damaged in a bombing raid during the last war and was never re-opened.

The QUEEN'S HALL THEATRE, Edward Street, The Parade.

Opened in early 1909. Proprietors and Managers J.P. Moore and B. Kennedy, who also ran the "Kings Hall" in Corporation Street. It only lasted a few months showing Vaudeville and Concerts and Animated Pictures. In October 1909 it was taken over by the Birmingham Arena Limited under the management of John Roberts and opened on the 11th October as "The Birmingham New House of Boxing". This too only lasted a few months. In 1910 it opened as The Queen's Picture house under the management of Walter Payne. After refurbishment it opened as The Lyric Cinema on 22nd Sept. 1919. It closed on 10th October 1960. The building was demolished in 1985. Prior to opening as a theatre it was the Church of Christ the Saviour, built by George Dawson, M.A. in 1847.

The COTTERIDGE PICTUREDROME and VARIETY THEATRE, situated in Hudson's Drive, off Pershore Road, Cotteridge.

Opened in 1911 showing a variety of exciting acts that were much appreciated by patrons. It had a seating capacity of 480. It gave twice nightly performances, 6.50 and 7.30 p.m. It was under the management of Mr. F.W.Pullen. It closed c 1920.

Advertisement in Midland Music Halls publication August 1913.

4th March 1914.

TOWN HALL, Victoria Square.

Opened in October 1834, architect Joseph Aloysius Hansom. It was a prominent venue for all forms of entertainment. In 1846 Mendolssohn, the German musical composer of oratorios, concert-overtues etc., made a personal appearance presented his production of "Elijah", specially written for the occasion and conducted by himself. This was a memorable occasion. In 1907 George Halford gave his ninth annual concert (see notice) price of admission one shilling. Uncle John Charities gave annual Christmas Party Concerts and on January 7th 1913 presented their ninth.

Miss Joyce Barbour, Miss Demaine and Mr. Johnny Woods gave performances by kind permission of Louis Salberg from the Alexandra Theatre. Presentation of Prizes to the most successful collectors for the Fund was given by the Right Hon. the Lord Mayor of Birmingham (Col. E. Martineau). The charity was started by the young readers of the Children's Corner of the Birmingham Weekly Post. 500 children were entertained at this event.

The Town Hall Organ, built in 1834 by William Hill, was completey re-built in 1983-84 and was re-opened on the 6th October 1984 in time for the 150th Anniversary of the Hall. George Thalben-Ball was the City organist period 1949-1982. The present organist is Thomas Trotter. Lunch time concerts are organised by him at the present time, mostly on Wednesdays.

The City of Birmingham Symphony Orchestra (C.B.S.O.), as it is today, commenced in 1944, its director up to the early 1950's was Rudolf Schwarz, he was succeeded by George Weldon. The present conductor is Simon Rattle C.B.E.

The City of Birmingham Choir, was founded in 1921 and chiefly performs with the C.B.S.O. when they present a series of annual concerts in the hall. The present conductor is Christopher Robinson. One of these is the Christmas Concert held in December, always to a packed audience.

Town Hall, Birmingham,

THE HALFORD CONCERTS SOCIETY
(Musical Director: Mr. George Halford)

Orchestral Concert

JANUARY 30, 1906.

ORCHESTRA OF EIGHTY PERFORMERS.
Leader: Mr. Ernst Schiever.

Conductor: Mr. George Halford.

Overture, "Hebrides" ... Mendelssohn
Violin Concerto ... ...
Symphony of "Irish" Hamilton Harty
Serenade for Wind, op. 7 ... ... Strauss
Varsang (Song of Spring) ... ... Sibelius

VIOLINIST:

Mr. Fritz Kreisler.

Tickets and Plan of Seats at Messrs. Priestley and Sons, Colmore Row, Birmingham, where annotated Programmes, with musical illustrations, price Sixpence, can also be obtained ten days in advance of each concert.

The Concert commences punctually at 8 p.m, and terminate about 9-45.

For Single Concert: Reserved Galleries, 6/-,
Reserved back of Great Gallery, 3/6,
Unreserved Seats, 2/- and 1/-,
The whole of Floor will be Unreserved,
Admission, 2/- and 1/-.

TOWN HALL. BIRMINGHAM.

GRAND CONCERT

PATRON:—
THE RIGHT HON. THE LORD MAYOR OF BIRMINGHAM,

WILL BE HELD ON

WEDNESDAY, MARCH 14, 1906,

In connection with the Welsh Church Choir, Suffolk Street.

Miss **MAY JOHN**, the eminent Soprano; Miss **MARY HUGHES**, of the London Queen's Hall and Provincial Concerts (first appearance in Birmingham of the distinguished Welsh soprano, who had the honour to appear before H.R.H. the Prince of Wales); **Mr. SETH HUGHES** (by the kind permission of Paul A. Rubens, Esq., Apollo Theatre, London).

Accompanist, Mrs. W. C. Roberts.

Conductor ... ... **Mr. TOM GRIFFITHS.**

Prices of Admission:— 2/6, 1/6, and 1/-

Doors open at 7-50. Concert to commence at 8. Carriages, 10-15.

Town Hall, Birmingham,

THE HALFORD CONCERTS SOCIETY
(Musical Director: Mr. George Halford)

Orchestral Concert

MARCH 13th, 1906.

ORCHESTRA OF EIGHTY PERFORMERS.
Leader: Mr. Ernst Schiever.

Conductor: Mr. George Halford.

Overture, "Hansel und Gretel"...Humperdinck
Violin Concerto .. ... Tschaikowsky
Symphony, "Tragic" ... ... Schubert
Capriccio-Espagnol ... Rimsky Korsakoff

VIOLINIST:

Mr. Zacharewitsch.

Tickets and Plan of Seats at Messrs. Priestley and Sons, Colmore Row, Birmingham, where annotated Programmes, with musical illustrations, price Sixpence, can also be obtained ten days in advance of each concert.

The Concert commences punctually at 8 p.m, and terminate about 9-45.

For Single Concert: Reserved Galleries, 6/-,
Reserved back of Great Gallery, 3/6,
Unreserved Seats, 2/- and 1/-,
The whole of Floor will be Unreserved,
Admission, 2/- and 1/-.

TOWN HALL, BIRMINGHAM.

NINTH

HALFORD

ORCHESTRAL

CONCERT

Tuesday, March 26th,

AT 8.

VOCALIST:
MADAME

ADA CROSSLEY,

Who will sing—

"SEA PICTURES" .... Elgar
CANTATA "SCHLAGE DOCH" Bach

Mr. COLERIDGE TAYLOR
will conduct his new work—
"VARIATIONS ON AN AFRICAN AIR,"
For Orchestra.

ORCHESTRA OF 80 PERFORMERS,
Conductor—

MR. GEORGE HALFORD.

Doors open at 7-30. Concert at 8 p.m.

Carriages at 10 p.m.

Tickets: 6s., 5s., 4s., 2s.

ADMISSION: - ONE SHILLING.

The Birmingham Weekly Post.

"UNCLE JOHN'S" CHARITIES.

This unique philanthropic movement was the first charity in this country organised by children in aid of children. It was started by the young readers of the Children's Corner of the "Weekly Post" over seventeen years ago, under the leadership of "Uncle John," and each year the funds raised by these young Busy Bees suffice to give a big Xmas Party to poor children in the Town Hall, besides sending each year some hundreds of sickly children to recuperate in country cottages. In addition Uncle John's nephews and nieces have established a "Weekly Post" Cot at the Children's Hospital, and have endowed it permanently. They have also endowed an Uncle John Cot at the Convalescent Home of the Birmingham Crippled Children's Union and have now an emigration branch connected with the Middlemore Homes. These charities have, moreover, the merit that all the funds raised are applied intact to the objects for which they are intended without deduction for expense of administration.

PROGRAMME

"Birmingham Weekly Post."

TWENTY-FIFTH ANNUAL
UNCLE JOHN'S
POOR CHILDREN'S

Christmas Party

TOWN HALL

(Kindly granted by the Lord Mayor, Alderman Byng Kenrick)

FRIDAY, JANUARY 18th, 1929

Given by

"Members of the Children's Corner."

Chairman - GEORGE JACKSON, Esq., J.P.

Doors open at 4.45 p.m.   Tea at 5 p.m.

- PROGRAMME -

Songs and Comic Interludes by Artistes of Alexandra Theatre Pantomime
"Dick Whittington."

By kind permission of Mr. Leon Salberg, Proprietor.

Selections by .. THE SHENLEY FIELDS BOYS' HOME BAND,
By kind permission of the Committee

Comedy and Dance Act .. .. NIECE OLWEN LUDLOW

Comic Variety Act .. .. .. THE WALKER TWINS

Fancy Dance and Song Act THE PUPILS OF MADAME WINIFRED HOLT

An Interlude of Magic .. .. .. MR. DANIELS

Humorous Scena—"Safety First," including the song, "Seymour Safety" .. .. MESSRS. TEDDY WALKER and FRED CECIL

Song and Dance .. NEPHEW JACK COOPER and LITTLE JOAN

Juvenile Comedy Act .. MASTER ALLENBY GUEST and NIECE EVA BELL

Comedy Act .. .. MR. J. H. MASTERS

Presentation of Prizes by the Lord Mayor
to the most successful Collectors for the Fund

Popular Music .. .. .. THE SHENLEY FIELDS BAND

Humorous Sketch   MR. W. CLAYTON & LITTLE BETTY CLAYTON

Costume Dance .. .. .. LITTLE BETTY FOX

Comedy Act .. .. .. THE WALKER TWINS

Community Song (all to join in Chorus)—"Land of Hope and Glory,"
Led by MR. EDWARD RABY

"God Save the King" .. .. .. Led by MR. RABY

Honorary Pianist   MR. BERT CADBY

DISTRIBUTION OF PRIZES to the young
Guests on leaving the Hall by Santa Claus.

THE UNCLE JOHN MATINEE,
GRAND THEATRE : : BIRMINGHAM
ABOUT THE END OF FEBRUARY.

Uncle John's Community Ball
TONY'S BALLROOM, HURST STREET
NEXT THURSDAY.
Tickets at "Weekly Post" Office, New Street.

57

AMPHITHEATRE, Livery Street, Birmingham.

Was opened c 1787 as a Gentlemans Private Theatre. It was a spacious building some 140 feet long and 54 feet wide. It was only operative until 1790 when, on the 30th of August it was put up for sale having Dressing Rooms, Offices, Boxes, Pit, Gallery, Circus, Stage, Orchestra and Scenery. Seating for around 2000. Membership was by annual subscription. The building was demolished in 1848.

AMPHITHEATRE, Stork Tavern Yard, situated at the rear of the Stork Tavern Inn in the Old Square, Birmingham.

Opened in 1802 showing circus and variety acts and later dramatic shows. It was only operative a few years and closed c 1806. Prices of admission, Boxes 3/-, Pit 2/-, Gallery 1/- Standing Places 6d.

BASKERVILLE HALL, Cambridge Street.

In November 1885 the Sheridan Dramatic Company put on a performance entitled "Waiting for the Verdict". The play was well received. The principal parts were played by Mr. J. Clare — Blinkey Brown, Mr. W. Edgington — Jonas Hurdle, Mr. A. Mowbry — Humphrey Hisson, and Mr. G. Roden — Lieut. Florville. An excellent performance was given by Miss C. Graham. Variety entertainment followed by two of the best comics of the day — McKenna and O'Connell.

BARNES CONCERT HALL, Sherbourne Place, Sherbourne Road, Moseley.

Opened in 1866 by Tommy Barnes, this could have been the first suburban Concert Hall to be opened at this time. Prices of admission 6d, performance started at 7.30 p.m. It was adjacent to the Royal Hotel and formed part of the St. Helena Gardens. On the 17th October 1887 Mr. E. Martin was appointed manager of the concert hall and the hotel, it changed its name to Sherbourne Concert Hall, he ran it until 1890 at a considerable financial loss, hence its closure.

CONCERT BOOTH and OPERA HOUSE, Moseley Road, Highgate.

This was an elegant wooden building erected near Leopold Street junction in 1778. It advertised a programme of Concert of Vocal and Instrumental Music. Artists from the Theatre Royal in Covent Garden, London appeared there. Prices of admission, Boxes 3/-, Pit 2/-, Gallery 1/-. Sadly the building burned down on the 14th August the same year it opened.

GEORGE and DRAGON CONCERT HALL, situated on the corner of Weaman Street and Steelhouse Lane.

Opened c 1840. It is said to be the first Music Hall to be opened in Birmingham. The Evening Mail and Birmingham Post now occupies this site.

JUNCTION CONCERT HALL, corner of Wheeler Street and Great King Street.

Was operative in 1885. It was part of the Junction Inn. On Tuesday 8th December 1885 a benefit was held for the celebrated Irish comedian Peter Roach. Mr. Wallace Winkles, the proprietor, made a very handsome present to Mr. Roach.

MINOR THEATRE, Worcester Street, City centre.

This was indeed a minor theatre and was only operative a few years. It was opposite the King's Head Inn. Opened in 1818 and closed in 1821.

PALACE OF DELIGHT, Bristol Street.

Opened in 1896, William Coutts was the Managing Director and the Sole Proprietor. It opened with the showing of a pantomime, this was followed by popular plays of the period which included 'Trilby' by Paul Potter and the drama, 'East Lynne'. Prices of admission 1s, 6d, 4d and 2d. The following year the Justices in Birmingham would not renew his licence on the grounds that the building contained too much wood and was a fire hazard. Mr. Coutts was a kind and considerate man and his ambition was to bring brightness and happiness into the heart of the people of Birmingham. He organised outings for poor children and put on Musical and Lantern Services on Sundays. He also arranged free Sunday morning breakfasts for the poor children in connection with Mr. Pentland's Street Robins Movement. Bristol Street Motors is now operating on this site.

The ROYAL STANDARD CONCERT HALL, Golden Cup Inn, 37 Smallbrook Street.

Opened in 1860 but was only operative for a very short time.

Proprietor J. Swan. Lessee H. Roberts. It was advertised as a Commodious Concert Hall having talented artists in their several professorships direct their efforts to amuse, delight and instruct their audience. Admission Free. Open every evening in the week, at half past seven. Organist and Pianist Mr. H. Barton.

RYAN'S AMPHITHEATRE and NEW GRAND ARENA, Bradford Street, Bordesley.

This was erected in 1827 and after enlargement and alterations in 1838 was renamed Amphitheatre. In 1842 it was again renamed, this time to Dicrow's Circus, it only lasted a few years and then became the Circus Baptist Chapel in 1849. In 1895 the City Meat Market & Slaughter House was erected on this site.

ST. JAMES HALL, 14 Snow Hill, opposite Snow Hill Station.

Opened in 1868 and gave a variety of performances. It had a seating capacity of around 700, building consisted of ground floor and balcony. It had a variety of owners and over the years was used for various forms of entertainment. In 1913 it was the Egyptian Hall Billiard Rooms, it had 14 tables, was open all day and charged 1/- per hour.

The THEATRE, Smallbrook Street c 1747-1750.

In the May publication of "Aris's Gazette" in 1747 the play, "The Earl of Essex" and the Celebrated entertainment of the "Harelequin's Vagaries" was reported, they played to a crowded audience. Price of admission 2/6, 2/-, 1/- and 6d.

The UNICORN INN and CONCERT HALL, 46 Digbeth, Birmingham.

Opened c 1885 presenting a variety of programmes for patrons. It was under the management of E.G. Goldsmith who was for several years the manager of the London Museum and Concert Hall.

BOTANICAL GARDENS, Edgbaston.

These gardens opened on 11 June 1832, the Exhibition and Concert Hall was erected and opened on the 13 May 1885. The W.C. Stockley's String Orchestra was engaged to play from 2.30 p.m. onwards. Prices of admission 2/6 on this special day. Concerts have been held here from time to time. Period 1887-1890 a series of theatrical performances were organised by Ben Greet of the Haymarket Theatre, London, normally on a wooden stage erected in the grounds. The Exhibition Hall was enlarged in 1894 and entertainment has increased with performances by Military Bands and Vocal Concerts. The hall was completely refurbished in 1987.

Those famous old music hall songs:-

All the Nice Gilrs Love a Sailor
  Boiled Beef and Carrots
    Fall in and Follow Me
      Who Were you With Last Night
       Man on the Flying Trapeze
        Bill Bailey, Won't You Come Home
         I Do Like to be Beside the Seaside
          Hold your Hand out, you Naughty Boy
         Ta-Ra-Ra Boom-de-ay
          Where Did you get that Hat
        Glorious Beer

Oh' Oh' Antonio
  Here we are, Here we are, Here we are again
    Jolly Good Luck to the Girl who loves a Soldier
   Down at the Old Bull and Bush
   Don't Dilly Dally on the Way
     She's a Lassie from Lancashire
      Hello' Hello' Who's your Lady Friend
    Ship Ahoy!
      Just a Wee Doch and Doris
        How Ya Gonna Keep 'em down on the Farm
       I Can't do my Bally Bottom Button Up
        Sister Susie's Sewing Shirts for Soldiers
        Daddy Wouldn't buy me a Bow-Wow
      Waiting at the Church
      Flanagan
        She Sells Sea Shells
         After the Ball was over
        K-K-K Katy

Following in Father's Footsteps
  In the Shade of the Old Apple Tree
    I Wouldn't Leave my Little Wooden Hut for You!
    I'm Henry the Eighth I am
     When Father Papered the Parlour
      He'd Have to get under, Get out and Get Under
     Waiting for the Robert E. Lee
    When I leave the World Behind
      Somewhere, the Sun is Shining
     Ask a Policeman
       The Man who broke the Bank at Monte Carlo
      After the Ball was Over
      Burlington Bertie

If you were the only Girl in the World
  If it wasn't for the 'Ouses in Between
   It's a Long Way to Tipperary
    Show me the Way to go Home
     Oh' Oh' Antonio
      Has anybody here seen Kelly
     The Miner's Dream of Home
    Burlington Bertie
      A Little bit of what you fancy does you good
      The Boy I love is up in the Gallery
     Champagne Charlie
     Broken Doll
      Lily of Laguna
     Comrades
      Smilin' Through
       For Old Times Sake

To name but a few!

The ODEON CONCERT THEATRE,
New Street.

It was originally The Paramount Theatre which opened on the 4th September, 1937. It changed it's name to 'Odeon' in August 1942, when it was taken over by the Rank Organisation. It closed in 1965 for major modernisation costing £70,000. It re-opened on the 25th of June showing the film "Genghis Khan", this was preceded by the stage appearance of Cliff Richard and The Shadows. The Lord Mayor of Birmingham was present, Alderman H.C. Taylor together with other civic dignitaries. The manager was Leslie J. Harris. This was the beginning of showing live shows which gradually built up over the years to be the leading Midland Concert Venue for 'POP'. 1982 was the busiest year showing over 150 concerts. The final concert was given on the 9th July 1987 by "The Count Basie Orchestra". It proved to be a great night of jazz. There was a lot of opposition to its closure as a concert venue but it has now reverted back to a normal cinema. The General Manager was Chris. Mott, F.I.E.M. and the entrepreneur was Doris Stokes.

On Sunday 6th September 1987 it celebrated its 50th anniversary, a special nostalgic film show was put on, which included a 1936 PATHE Pictorial film. The now famous Compton Organ swung into action and instrumentalists who had been invited to appear included Charles Smitton, Ron Curtiss, Joe Marsh, Eddie Rihier, Foley Bates and the resident organist, Steven Tovey.

Doris Stokes, the entrepreneur and Chris Mott the General Manager.

The **MIDLANDS ARTS CENTRE,** Cannon Hill Park, Birmingham B12 9QH.

This was established in 1962, it is operated by the Cannon Hill Trust, the director is Robert Pretty. It was pioneered by John English and Alicia Randle. It started life as the Midlands Art Centre for Young People, the 'For young People' was dropped some years ago and it now includes all age groups.

The Centre possesses a Studio Theatre which was opened by Princess Margaret in 1965, the play selected was, "The Servant of Two Masters", directed by John English. It also has a "Puppet Theatre", director John M. Blundel, Administrator Carolyn Bettis. Its aim is both to entertain and to stimulate the creative impulses of young children.

The completion of major refurbishment, which cost ½ million pounds, was completed in October 1987 and was officially launched on the 17th of October. This included the opening of a new Cinema seating 150, the film selected was "Business as Usual" (an apt title) starring Glenda Jackson and John Thaw, and licensed bar, courtyard development and extensions to the restaurant. The cinema was opened by the director of the film shown, Lezli-An Barrett.

The Centre is also the centre for Craftspace, a craft gallery and touring exhibition service which was founded by the West Midlands Arts and Crafts Council. It is also a permanent base for the Central Junior Television Workshop and the City of Birmingham Touring Opera (an amalgamation of Birmingham Music Theatre). MAC is well worth a visit. It is 'Marvellous and Cosy'. The entrance is via Queen's Ride.

The MOSELEY and BALSALL HEATH INSTITUTE, Moseley Road, Balsall Heath.

This was founded in 1876. The Hall was built in 1883 by money subscribed and raised by voluntary efforts on land presented by the Misses Lawrence. Dramatic performances and Concerts have been performed over the years. It was the venue for the local dramatic group, 'The Moseley Players'. Period 3rd to 11th of February 1953 the Birmingham Drama Festival was presented showing 3 to 4 plays nightly. The adjudicator was Maxwell Wray. The stage is fully equipped with a comprehensive lighting and sound equipment. It is a popular local venue.

The BIRMINGHAM THEATRE CENTRE.

Officially opened on 23rd November 1957 and raised a considerable interest in both the professional and amateur dramatic circles. It was the outcome of an agreement between the Birmingham Civic Authority and the Birmingham & District Theatre Guild, of which W. Bushill-Matthews M.B.E., was the Executive Committee Chairman. The play selected was, "Old Wine — New Bottle".

The Lord Mayor of Birmingham, Councillor J.J. Grogan, M.B.E. was present and also Sir Donald Wolfit and Sir Barry Jackson as guests of honour. It had a seating capacity of 200 but, as 600 attended the function, three official opening ceremonies had to be performed. The stage lighting was presented by the Charles Henry Foyle Trust, and funds had been aided by the "Seats with a Memory" scheme, to which many celebrities of stage, screen and radio had contributed. A seat then bore their names. The red plush seats had been purchased from the Theatre Royal in New Street, before it was demolished in December 1956.

The building was demolished in the early 1970's due to a road widening scheme and the centre was transferred to the Old Repertory Theatre in Station Street. The building was originally the Old Edgbaston Vestry Hall.

The CRESCENT THEATRE LIMITED.

When this theatre originally opened, it was run by amateur theatrical enthusiasts, known as the Municipal players, membership was restricted to council employees and teachers. They took over a derelict warehouse on the corner of Cambridge Street and The Crescent No.18. It was officially opened on the 8th April 1932 by the Lord Mayor of Birmingham, Sir John Burman. The play selected was, "The Romantics" by Edmond Rostand. They moved to the new premises in Cumberland Street in October 1964. The Players were originally formed in 1923.

THE CRESCENT THEATRE LIMITED

Cumberland Street, Birmingham B1 2JA.
T. 021 643 5858/9

Public Theatre. Company Established 1923.
Theatre Established 1932. New Theatre opened 1964.

President	David Pinell
Chairman	Ron Barber, 10 Don Close, Augustus Road, Birmingham B15 3PN. T. 021 455 7832.
Secretary	Jenni Milward, 43 Northfield Road, Kings Norton, Birmingham B31 1JD. T. 021 451 3368.
Treasurer	David Newman, Bank House, 1 York Road, Hall Green, Birmingham B28 3BD. T. 021 778 5294.
Art Manager	George Harrison, 73 Overbury Close, Birmingham B31. T. 021 477 5673.
Production	Sue Steele, 12 Lady Greys Walk, Wollaston, Stourbridge, DY8 3RD. T. 0384 376043.
LTGC	May Small, 'The Barn', Southam Road, Hall Green, Birmingham, B28 0AB. T. 021 777 2043.

Charity Reg. No. 254054
Productions 9
Performances 13
Seating capacity 296
Stage: Pros. opening
8.5.16.0m
Pros. height
3.4–4.4m
Depth 9.1m
Wing space
Variable 0–3.6m
Other activities AE PR WH
MG YG
Prompt. P
Bar (Theatre Licence)

Productions (Seats £2.80, OAPs £1.80)

The Exorcism	Don Taylor
Othello	William Shakespeare
Gaslight and Garters	Crescent Theatre
Aladdin	Brian Butler (Crescent)
Hitch Hiker's Guide to the Galaxy	Douglas Adams
Spring and Port Wine	Bill Naughton
Rosencrantz and Guildenstern are Dead	Tom Stoppard
Privates on Parade	Peter Nichols
The Country Wife	William Wycherley

1985

by Ray Cooney and John Chapman

5th – 19th
SEPTEMBER
1987
AT 7.30 pm

"A riotous farce...
so funny it hurts!"

CRESCENT THEATRE
CUMBERLAND STREET (OFF BROAD STREET) BIRMINGHAM B1 2JA.
BOX OFFICE: 021-643 5858
TICKETS ALSO AVAILABLE FROM THE TICKET SHOP 021-643 2514

1982-83 SEASON

Sat 11th September-Sat 25th September
BORN IN THE GARDENS
PETER NICHOLS

Sat 23rd October-Sat 6th November
THE LADY FROM MAXIMS
(FEYDEAU) Trans. JOHN MORTIMER

Sat 11th-18th December Sat 1st-15th January
PETER PAN
J.M. BARRIE

Sat 29th January-Sat 5th February
ROSE
ANDREW DAVIES

Sat 26th February-Sat 12th March
THE COMEDIANS
TREVOR GRIFFITHS

Sat 23rd April-Sat 7th May
CHICAGO*
FRED EBB & BOB FOSSE

Sat 4th June-Sat 18th June
CAT ON A HOT TIN ROOF
TENNESSEE WILLIAMS

Sat 9th July- Sat 23rd July
PIAF
PAM GEMS

All performances start at 7.30pm
Price and booking details from Box Office   *Subject to availability

---

TICKET PRICES
FOR ALL CRESCENT THEATRE PRODUCTIONS
MONDAYS: All seats £2.00 each.
TUESDAYS to SATURDAYS: All seats £3.00 each.
Senior Citizens: £2.00 each (Except Saturdays).
PARTIES OF 20 OR MORE: £2.00 each
(Tuesday to Friday only).

BOOKING
The Box Office (021-643 5858) will be open for
personal and telephone bookings as follows:
MONDAY and THURSDAY evening from
6.30 to 8.30pm. (Closed on Bank Holidays).
PERFORMANCE NIGHTS from 6.30 to 8.30pm.

Postal bookings for any production in the season are
accepted at any time.
Tickets are also available at the Ticket Shop,
City Arcade, Birmingham.
(During normal shopping hours).
Telephone: 021-643 2514.
Credit cards are accepted at the Ticket Shop
but we regret NOT at the Crescent Theatre.

SEATING PLAN

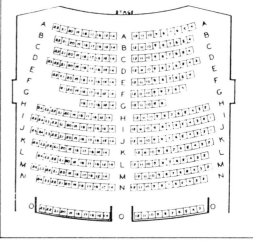

HIGHBURY LITTLE THEATRE, Sheffield Road, Sutton Coldfield.

This theatre was built by voluntary labour and opened in June 1942 as a Private Members Theatre. In 1946-47 membership was open to members of the public. Registration fee being £1.10.

The group of theatrical enthusiasts who built this theatre worked together for 12 years before the theatre was built. On Sunday 27th April 1924 they held their first meeting. They were known as The Highbury Players. The first stage appearance was given on the 5th March 1925. Plays were normally staged in the Folk House, Erdington and later in the Church House, also in Erdington. Rehearsals were held at the home of Mr. and Mrs. B.C. English at their home named, 'Highbury'. It was from this that the players and theatre took its name.

HIGHBURY THEATRE CENTRE LIMITED

Highbury Little Theatre, Sheffield Road,
Sutton Coldfield, West Midlands,
B73 5HD. T. 021 373 2761.

Private Theatre. Group Established 1924.
Theatre Established 1942.

President	John English, MA OBE, 571 Chester Road, Sutton Coldfield. B73 5HU. T. 021 373 1961
Chairman	Mollie Randle
Secretary	Mrs. Anne Reid, 215 Green Lanes, Sutton Coldfield.
Treasurer	Noel Sherwood, 5 Church Road, Shenstone, Lichfield. WS14 ON9. T. 0543 481162.
LTGC	Connie Grainger, 143 Chipstead Road, Birmingham, B23 5EY. T. 021 632 4199.

Productions (Seats £1.40)   % capacity

Hay Fever	Noel Coward	79
Can't Pay? Won't Pay!	Dario Fo	77
The Ugly Duckling	John English	94
A Trip to Scarborough	Arthur Miller	86
* Songs for a Summer Day	Keith Miles	81

* World Premiere

Youth Theatre

Kippers and Curtains	Devised by the Group
The Mystery of the Magic Marmalade	Devised by the Group
Double Bill- The Lucky Ones	
Raspberry	Tony Marchant

Charity Reg. No. 223923
Productions 6
Performances 10
Seating capacity 110
Stage: Pros. opening 4.7m
Pros. height 3.5m
Depth 6.4m
Wing space P 1.8m
OP 1.2m
Other activities AE PR WH
YG HPC
Bar (Club Licence)

1985

SUTTON ARTS THEATRE, South Parade, Sutton Coldfield.

This was founded in 1945 and for the first 9 years performed in Sutton Town Hall. In 1954 the present building was leased from the Sutton Borough and since then successive Management Committees have endeavoured to improve the facilities offered for the benefit of patrons.

The present Committee has embarked on one of the most ambitious projects since the building of the Auditorium, the erection of a Studio Theatre with additional workshop and storage space.

New members are always welcome, full details of membership can be obtained from the membership secretary, Lynne Wesley-Harkcome. Tel. No. 021 308 4285.

SUTTON ARTS THEATRE

South Parade, Sutton Coldfield, West Midlands, B72 1QU. T. 021 345 4256.
Box Office T. 021 355 5355.

Membership Theatre. Company Established 1945.
Theatre Established 1953.

President	Stuart Browning
Chairman	John Daniels
Secretary & LTGC	C. Arthur Jones, 2 Dunton Close, Sherifoot Lane, Sutton Coldfield B75 5QD. T. 021 308 0574.
Treasurer	Eileen Crow
Arts Directorate Chairman	Hilary Dorman, 299 Monmouth Drive, Sutton Coldfield B73 6JU. T. 021 345 5484.

Productions

Productions		% capacity
Quiet Weekend	E. McCracken	97 (8)
Betrayal	H. Pinter	97
See How They Run	P. King	99 (8)
On Golden Pond	E. Thompson	100
84 Charing Cross Road	H. Hanff (ad. J. Roose Evans)	100 (6)
Anastasia	M. Maurette	99
The Comedy of Errors	Shakespeare	97

The plays this past year offered a particularly unusual contrast in style and balance and were received with great satisfaction by audiences.

Productions 7
Performances 7
Seating capacity 124
Stage: Pros. opening 6.1m
　　　(can be extended to 8.2m)
　　　Pros. height 2.6m
　　　Depth 7.6m
　　　Wing space P 1.2m
　　　OP 1.2m
Other activities AE PR WH
Wednesday night club
HPC
Bar (Club Licence)

1985

Hall Green Little Theatre Limited

Pemberley Road, Acocks Green, Birmingham B27 7RY   Telephone (evenings): 021-706 1541

REGISTERED AS A CHARITY – No. 251575

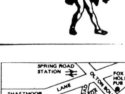

President: Lord Olivier
Vice Presidents: Norman C. Davis, A.R.I.B.A.
                  Sir Reginald Eyre, M.P.
                  W.G. Bushill Matthews, M.B.E.
                  John E. Payne, J.P.
                  Derek S. Salberg, C.B.E., J.P.

Chairman   Alan Moore, 118 Wychwood Avenue, Knowle,
             Solihull, B93 9DH. T. 021 560 4494.

Secretary   Mrs. Julia Roden, 12 Ridge Close, Kings
             Heath, Birmingham, B13 0EA. T. 021 777 2121.

Treasurer   Mrs. Sylvia Walton, 517 Oswio Court,
             Stratford Road, Shirley, Solihull B90 4AJ.
             T. 021 745 1580.

LTGC   Miss M. Whitehouse, 100 Stonor Road,
             Hall Green, Birmingham, B28 0QS. T. 021 744 3594.

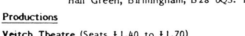

Productions   % capacity

Veitch Theatre (Seats £1.40 to £1.70)
California Suite   Neil Simon   68   Charity Reg. No. 251575
The Owl and the Pussy Cat   David Wood   86   Productions 7 (Veitch)
Educating Rita   Willy Russell   93   Productions 4 (Signature)
Heartbreak House   George Bernard Shaw   63   Performances 9 (Veitch)
Little Mary Sunshine   Rick Besoyen   80   Performances 5 (Signature)
The Daughter In Law   D. H. Lawrence   53   Seating capacity 202
Outside Edge   Richard Harris   83   Stage: Pros. opening 7.9m
                                                                    Pros. height 4.2m
Signature Theatre (Seats £1.25)   Depth 6.4m
Elephant Man   Bernard Pomerance   67   Wing space P 3m
The Farndale Avenue   OP 3m
Estate Townswomen's Guild   Other activities WH Script
Drama Society   Hire
Murder Mystery   McGillivray & Zerlin   97   Bar (Theatre Licence)
Joe Egg   Peter Nichols   39
The Hollow Crown   devised by John Barton 34

We are indebted to Hall Green Lions this year for providing us with a
continuous loop system for the hard of hearing. They bought and installed it
at no cost to ourselves.

1985

70

'The Veitch' Theatre auditorium.

HALL GREEN LITTLE THEATRE, Pemberley Road, Acocks Green.

This was founded by R.G. Taylor and opened on the 7th April 1951, just one year and one week after the commencement of building on land leased from the City. A building licence was granted on the understanding that no paid labour should be used, in the difficult building days just after the war years. The opening ceremony was performed by the Deputy Lord Mayor of Birmingham, Alderman Hubert Humphries J.P. The Chairman was D.N. Veitch. The play selected was, "The Circle of Chalk" by Klabund and produced by Keith A. Pickering (who was also the secretary). Assistant producer Alan Moore. Prior to the presentation of this performance a film was shown, "Greasepaint and Girders", made by Frank Atkinson and showing just how the theatre was built entirely by members. (see photographs). This was later transferred to Super 8 film with a commentary written by Alan Moore.

On the 30th March 1972, to celebrate its 21st birthday, the play, "The Relapse" by Sir John Vanbrugh was presented and produced by Alan Moore.

It was enlarged in 1981 and the Signature Theatre and bar were opened, this was known as Act II extension and was opened on the 30th March 1981 by Derek Salberg, C.B.E., J.P. The main auditorium was named, "Veitch Theatre".

It is a member of the Little Theatre Guild of Great Britain. Seven full length plays, and a number of others in the Signature Theatre, are presented each season. There are two classes of membership, active and audience. Active membership is open to actors, actresses, technicians, front of house staff. Full details of audience membership can be obtained from the present secretary, Julia Roden. The theatre has an extensive wardrobe, costumes and props, which are available for hire at reasonable prices.

Highspot in the first half of the theatre history was the granting of a licence and granting of Charity Status. It operates as a private theatre club but, membership is open to anyone. It is a company limited by guarantee as from 1956.

In 1981 a group was formed, "Friends of HGLT". Chairman Hugh Roden, secretary Tony Parsons. Their object is to raise funds for the theatre and help out whenever necessary.

Building Process.

It's sell-out already

Hall Green Little Theatre's special production for children in its new Signature Theatre has already sold out — a month in advance.

The run of Old King Cole was increased by an additional two nights such was audience response. It now runs from November 17 to 27.

1982

1986/7 SEASON

Signature Theatre: Mon. 15th — Sat. 20th September 1986.
THE REAL INSPECTOR HOUND' by TOM STOPPARD.
Box Office opens Wed. 10th September.

Veitch Theatre: Thurs. 2nd — Sat. 11th October 1986.
'SAY GOODNIGHT TO GRANDMA' by COLIN WELLAND.
Box Office opens Wed. 24th September.

Signature Theatre: Mon. 3rd — Sat. 8th November 1986.
'THE KINGFISHER' by WILLIAM DOUGLAS HOME.
Box Office opens Wed. 29th October.

Veitch Theatre: Thurs. 27th November — Sat. 13th December 1986.
'THE ENCHANTED FOREST' by ANTHONY WOODHALL.
Box Office opens Wed. 19th November.

Veitch Theatre: Thurs. 22nd — Sat. 31st January 1987.
'SHOCK' by BRIAN CLEMENS.
Box Office opens Wed. 14th January.

Veitch Theatre: Thurs. 5th — Sat. 14th March 1987.
'ALPHABETIC ORDER' by MICHAEL FRAYN.
Box Office opens Wed. 25th February.

Signature Theatre: Mon. 30th March — Sat. 4th April 1987.
'SUDDENLY LAST SUMMER' by TENNESSEE WILLIAMS.
Box Office opens Wed. 25th March.

Veitch Theatre: Thurs. 23rd April — Sat. 2nd May 1987.
'SWEENEY TODD' by BRIAN BURTON.
Box Office opens Wed. 15th April.

Veitch Theatre: Thurs. 4th — Sat. 13th June 1987.
'DANGEROUS CORNER' by J.B. PRIESTLEY.
Box Office opens Wed. 27th May.

Signature Theatre: Mon. 29th June — Sat. 4th July 1987.
'THE RESISTIBLE RISE OF ARTURO UI' by BERTOLT BRECHT.
Box Office opens Wed. 24th June.

Veitch Theatre: Thurs. 23rd July — Sat. 1st August 1987.
'WHAT THE BUTLER SAW' by JOE ORTON.
Box Office opens Wed. 15th July.

President: Laurence Olivier. *Vice Presidents:* Derek S. Salberg C.B.E., Jack Payne J.P., W. Bushill-Mathews M.B.E., Sir Reginald Eyre M.P., Norman C. Davis A.R.I.B.A. *Chairman:* Tony Mullins.
Secretary: Julia Roden. *Treasurer:* Sylvia Walton. *Founder:* R.G. Taylor.

Hall Green Little Theatre Limited,
Pemberley Road, Birmingham B27 7RY. Telephone: 021-706 1541.

A scene from the play, "The Anniversary" by Bill Macilwraith, the 6th production in the 1982/3 season. Players from left to right, Steve Parsons, Julie Martin, Jean McClelland, Barbara Hunter and James Dowson.

A scene from the play, "Sleeping Beauty" by Betty Astell, the 2nd production in the 1983/4 season. Players, from left to right, back row Jessie Whittle, Jane Roberts, Roy Palmer, Kym Andrews, Alison Milne, front, Louise Price and Carolyn Jenkins.

The Lord Mayor and Lady Mayoress of Birmingham, Councillor and Mrs F.J.Grattidge attending on the 'Open Day' on Saturday 26th September 1987. Peter Allso on the left and Alan Moore on the right.

Hall Green Little Theatre
PEMBERLEY ROAD (OFF SHAFTMOOR LANE)

OPEN DAY

FREE TOURS BACKSTAGE

TOMBOLA   REFRESHMENTS

FREE! FILM SHOW "GREASEPAINT AND GIRDERS" (How we built a Theatre!)

FREE LIVE SHOW "Behind the Scenes"

BAR LUNCHTIME

BOOK SALE!

SCOUTS CAR WASH £1

COSTUME DISPLAYS

KID'S DRESSING UP CORNER with instant photos!

10AM TO 4PM
SATURDAY 26TH SEPTEMBER

1987

KINGS HEATH LITTLE THEATRE.

Founded in the early 1930's by Gina Manly, members were known as 'The Curtain Players'. They had no permanent premises but gave performances at a selection of premises in Birmingham and area. They were a happy band of 25 players.

The first performance was presented at the Midland Arts Fellowship, Theosophical Hall in Great Charles Street, Birmingham. Other venues, Moseley and Balsall Heath Institute, Bournville Concert Hall, The Community Centre in Trittiford Road, Yardley Wood, School premises and village halls. During the last war they entertained at Armed Forces Camps and Home Guard H.Q's., and at Hospitals for patients and staff. They also presented plays at Winson Green, Exeter and Dartmoor Prisons.

This is a scene from the play, "Castle in the Air", a comedy by Alan Melville, presented at Bournville Infants School in the 1956/7 season. Players from left to right, James Pratt, John Rutter and Gina Manly.

They present 6 plays per season. Their last play "Ladies in Retirement" (an apt title) was presented at the Baptist Church, High Street, Kings Heath in 1966.

The Kings Heath Little Theatre BEST WISHES 7th OCTOBER From DARTMOOR

There are '600' men upon "The Moor."
Who hope the 'cheers,' will raise the rafters
We know your plays will never bore.
And wish you luck in "Present Laughter."

Good luck to you all, in "Present Laughter"
From All the Men at Dartmoor & their Chaplain.
To Gina Manly (DIRECTOR)
And all the members of:–
The Kings Heath Little Theatre.

LOCAL ENTERTAINERS

THE ARDEN SINGERS. Director: William D.S. Bennett, b. June 1914 d. November 1985. ed. Kings Norton Secondary School, Birmingham.

Initially, a group of 12 girls from teens to twenties, formed in March, 1940 by W.D.S.B., who had previously directed a young mixed choir from 1936-39, called the Malvern Singers, whilst he was employed by Cadbury Bros. of Bournville, but this group had to be disbanded at the outbreak of the second world war when the male members were called up for service in H.M. Forces.

In the early years Arden Singers' rehearsals were held at the home of the Director but as their concerts increased more girls were recruited and their membership became 24. Eventually they moved their headquarters to 110 Bristol Road, Edgbaston, which was known as "Studio One".

Their popularity grew rapidly, as did their repertoire, which included light, classical and sacred music; all the songs being arranged into four-parts by W.D.S.B., and some to music of his own composition. They provided musical entertainment for H.M. Forces, charitable organisations, churches and masonic functions — and occasionally for Winson Green Prison!

Performances were given in many Midland theatres, town & civic halls, churches, and in the Queensbury Club, Birmingham, a venue for entertainment for service personnel stationed in or travelling through Birmingham. They went to London regularly to sing at the war-time famous Stage Door Canteen and in Variety Bandbox at the Coliseum. Many miles were travelled around the Midlands, and further afield engagements included Bournemouth, Folkestone, Rhyl, Devon and Isle of Wight.

As well as entertaining British Forces in war and peace time, they sang regularly for the American, Commonwealth, Dutch and Free French Units stationed in this country, and later, at some P.O.W. camps. Whilst in Britain, General de Gaulle personally presented the A.S. with a medal in appreciation of their singing for his troops.

In 1946 they were invited to go on a goodwill mission to the Hague, Holland, with a party of Midland sports men and women — the first to do so after the war. They stayed in the homes of the Dutch people and sang in several halls & theatres and broadcast from Radio Hilversum. Dutch songs were included in their concerts.

Both during and after the war the Singers took part in many B.B.C. broadcasts and one series from B.B.C. Broad Street, was a monthly event over about six months.

During all their years of singing a great amount of work was done for charity and many organisations and churches benefited from A.S. help. Over the years they appeared with many notable top singers, entertainers, orchestras and dance bands. In the later years of their existence much of this work was kept up and in the 60's and early 70's they also made some T.V. appearances and did more Radio work, particularly for B.B.C. children's programmes. They finally disbanded in 1972 when members were more difficult to recruit.

William Bennett died in November 1985 after a short illness, and in February 1986 a memorial concert was given in his memory at the Old Rep., in Station Street. About 30 former Arden Singers including several founder members, took part, along with representatives of other musical societies, bands, and drama personnel; all of them paying tribute to his work as a musical director, and as an Adjudicator at Music & Drama Festivals.

A reunion of Arden Singers now takes place in March each year.

Arden Singers at Dudley Town Hall c 1950.

Arden Singers c 1943.

The Harry Engleman Dance Orchestra, founded in 1936, appeared at numerous venues all over the Midlands and area and on T.V. from the Gosta Green studio.

"The DORCHESTER LOVELIES" a Birmingham Dancing troupe, one of the numerous troupes, trained by the Theatrical & Dancing Academy in Shirley Road, Acocks Green, Birmingham run by Jack & Joan Cooper both Birmingham born. They appeared at various venues in and around Birmingham.

THE BETTY FOX STAGE SCHOOL, 183 Bristol Road, Edgbaston.

The well known, 'Betty Fox Babes' were founded, at this school in 1938 and made their first appearance in pantomime at the Prince of Wales Theatre for Emile Littler this year. The pantomime was, 'Cinderella', it had a cast of 100. Elsie and Doris Walters played the ugly sisters and Tommy Trinder played 'Buttons'. This was the start of a long association with Emile Littler's productions in this country. During the last war the 'Babes' continued to appear each year in pantomimes.

They appeared in the 1987-88 season at the Alexandra Theatre in the pantomime, 'Dick Whittington' and this marked 50 years of the 'Babes' in pantomime.

Betty Dale Fox, A.R.A.D., M.I.S.T.D., took over the school from her aunt four years ago and it is still thriving.

BIRMINGHAM and MIDLAND INSTITUTE, Margaret Street, B3 3BS.

The Institute was constituted by an Act of Parliament of 3rd July 1854 for, "The Diffusion and Advancement of Science, Literature and Art". The foundation stone was laid by the Prince Consort in 1855. This building was then in Paradise Street next to the Town Hall, on the corner of Ratcliff Place. In 1869 Charles Dickens was president, in 1872 the office was held by Charles Kingsley, and in 1885 by E.W. Benson, Birmingham born, who was then the Archbishop of Canterbury.

On Tuesday 26th November 1907 the Union of Teachers and Students put on a Dramatic Performance of, "The School for Scandal", a comedy by R. Brinsley Sheridan, in the large lecture theatre. 7.00 p.m. for 7.30 p.m., admission one shilling. The stage manager was John S. Flavell.

The Shakespeare and Dramatic Society on the 82nd anniversary of the laying of the foundation stone at the Institute, presented on Saturday 20th November 1937 the play, "Mystery at Greenfingers", under the direction of E. Stuart Vinden. This play was specially written by J.B. Priestley for production by amateurs, with no thought of professional presentation, and, in addition, apart from its entertainment value, the play was witnessed by an adjudicator, who was to judge the merits of the performance in the novel, "News Chronicle Drama Competition". Artists taking part were Gladys Joiner as Mrs. Heaton, "Bobbie" Turner as Arnold Jordan, Archie Abbott as the Detective, and Lucy Griffiths (who made several appearances with Leon Salberg's Repertory Company at the Alexandra Theatre that season) in the part of Miss Tracey. Stage manager was W. Bushill-Matthews.

In 1965 the original building was demolished and the Institute moved to its present address.

The Institute has two theatres, the "Lyttelton Theatre", seating 300, and "The John Lee Theatre" seating 120, and two galleries for art exhibition besides smaller rooms suitable for rehearsals and social meetings.

The following societies are affiliated to the B.M.I. and hold regular meetings for their members, "The Villagers Drama Group" the B.M.I's own Drama Group, Midland Youth Orchestra, Birmingham School of Music Association, Second City Classical Guitar Society, M.D.C.C. Drama Group, The New Venturers Drama Co., Gilbert and Sullivan Society, the Savoy Operatic Society, The Dickens Fellowship and the Central Literary Association. Full details of membership of the B.M.I. can be obtained from the Hon. Secretary or by telephone on 021 236 3591. The Institute publishes a monthly magazine which is free of charge if collected, but which can be obtained by post for an annual subscription of £2.50.

ACTORS, ACTRESSES and THEATRICAL CELEBRITIES BORN IN BIRMINGHAM and AREA.

AHERNE, Brian, actor. Born 2 May 1902 in Kings Norton. Educated at Birmigham and Malvern College. Made his first stage appearance with the Pilgrim Players on the 5 April 1910 in "Fifinella". His first appearance in London was at the Garrick Theatre on 26 Dec. 1913 in "Where the Rainbow Ends", by Clifford Mills and John Ramsey. His first appearance on the New York stage at the Empire on 9 Feb. 1931 in "The Barretts of Wimpole Street" by Robert Browning. He commenced his film career in 1924 and became a well known film star.

ASHMORE, Basil, director. Born 13 September 1915 in Sutton Coldfield; formerly an actor who made his first stage appearance at the Birmingham Repertory Theatre in 1935. His first production "Hassan" by James Elroy Flecket, was presented at the Birmingham and Midland Institute in Paradise Street in 1937. He has broadcast frequently on a variety of subjects.

BARNES, Fred, musichall artist. Born in Birmingham in 1885. Made his first stage appearance in the pantomime "Cinderella" at the Alexandra Theatre in 1904. He also appeared at the Grand Theatre, The Empire, and Aston Hippodrome. He is especially remembered for his songs, "On Mother Kelly's Doorstep" and "The Black Sheep of the Family". He died in Southend on Sea on 23 October 1938 aged 53 years.

BARBOUR, Joyce, actress. Born 27 March 1901 in Birmingham. Made her first stage appearance in Birmingham, Christmas 1914 as a Fairy in a pantomime. Made her first appearance in London at the Gaiety Theatre on 28 April 1915 in the chorus of "To-night's the Night". Made numerous appearances at theatres all over this country and U.S.A. Appeared at the "Prince of Wales" Broad Street in June 1940 as Harriet Hastings in "Counter Attractions", she has also appeared in several films.

BAXTER, Beryl, actress. Born 9 April 1926 in Birmingham. Made her first stage appearance at the Shakespeare Memorial Theatre in Stratford upon Avon in 1943, as a fairy in "A Midsummer Night's Dream". First appeared in London at the Strand Theatre as Mary Biggleswade in, "Fifty Fifty", a farce by Larson Brown in 1946, this ran for over a year. She first appeared in films in 1947, in "The Idol of Paris".

BOOTH, Webster, actor and vocalist. Born 21 January 1902 in Birmingham. Educated at Lincoln Cathedral Choir and Aston Commercial School in Birmingham. Studied singing under Dr. Richard Wassell at Dale Forty's Studio in New Street, Birmingham. Made his first stage appearance at the Theatre Royal in Brighton on 9 September 1924 as the first Yeoman in "The Yeoman of the Guard" with the D'Oyley Carte Opera Co. First appeared in films in 1933. He made over 1000 broadcasts since 1928. Made his first TV appearance in 1930 from the BBC Studio in Gosta Green.

BRIGGS, Hedley, actor, producer, designer and dancer. Born 29 March 1907 in King's Norton. Educated at King Edward's School in Birmingham. Made his first stage appearance at the Birmingham Repertory Theatre on 29 October 1921 as Juanillo in, "Two Shepherds". He remained with this company as actor and assistant stage manager until 1926. His first London stage appearance was at the Regent Theatre, Kings Cross on 20 December 1922, as Colonel MacMashit and Harlequin in, "The Christmas Party". He served in the Royal Navy during the last war 1941-1945. He was commissioned in 1943.

BRITTON, Tony, actor. Born 9 June 1924 in Erdington. Educated Edgbaston Collegiate School, Hagley Road, Birmingham and Thombury Grammar School in Gloucestershire. First professional stage appearance, Knightstone Pavilion, Weston-Super-Mare in 1942. Appeared at the Alexandra Theatre, The New Repertory Theatre and the Birmingham Hippodrome.

BRYAN, Peggy, actress. Born in Birmingham 3 January 1916. Educated at Windermere College and the London Academy of Music and Drama. Was formerly a teacher of elocution at Highclare College in Sutton Coldfield. Made her first stage appearance in London at the Winter Garden Theatre as Puck in a scene from, "A Midsummer Night's Dream" at the Royal performance in aid of King George's Actors Pension Fund.

BYRNE, Cecily, actress. Born and educated in Birmingham. Made her first stage appearance with the Birmingham Repertory Theatre on 15 February 1913 in, "Twelfth Night", under the director of Barry V. Jackson, a relative. Her first London stage appearance was at the Ambassadors' Theatre on 6 February 1918 as Judith in, "The Little Brother". She was a very popular actress.

CARROLL, Madeleine, actress. Born 26 February 1906 in West Bromwich. Educated at the Birmingham University (obtained a BA.Hons, French) and on the Continent. Was a member of the Birmingham University Dramatic Society. Made her first stage appearance at the Winter Gardens Theatre, New Brighton in February 1927 as Jeanne in, "The Lash" by Cyril Campion. Went to the U.S.A. in 1936 and became a naturalised American citizen in 1943. Served in the American Red Cross during the last war and was awarded the Legion of Honour from the French Government. Commenced her film career in 1927. Died in October 1987 in Marbella, Spain.

CARROTT, Jasper, comedian. Born 14 March 1945 in Birmingham. Educated at Moseley Grammar School. Made his first professional appearance at the Masons Arms P.H. in Solihull in 1968. He has played at most of the major venues in the U.K. including the London Palladium and the Albert Hall and also in Australia, Hong Kong and the U.S.A. and also on T.V. and radio.

COOPER, G. Melville, actor. Born 15 October 1896 in Birmingham. Educated at King Edward's School in Birmingham. Made his first stage appearance in July 1914 at Stratford on Avon Memorial Theatre as the footman in, "The Return of the Prodigal" a comedy by St. John Hankin. After the First World War, in which he served, he joined the Birmingham Repertory Theatre and remained until 1924 playing many important parts. He has appeared in many films, the first one in 1934 and he has also appeared on T.V.

COSTELLO, Tom, comedian and music hall artist. Born 30 April 1863 in Birmingham. Made his first stage appearance at the Prince of Wales Theatre in Wolverhampton. Appeared at The London Museum Concert Hall in Birmingham in December 1895. He was a comedian of first rate ability. The songs he made famous were "Comrades", "At Trinity Church I met my Doom", "The Ship I Love" and "When the Old Church Bells are Ringing". He shared the top bill with stars like Dan Leno and Marie Lloyd. He earned about £80.00 per week which was a lot of money in those days. He died in Lambeth Hospital in London on 8 November 1943 aged 80 years.

CRATHORNE, Neville, illusionist. Born in Handsworth 6 June 1917. Educated at Greenmore College, Birmingham. Made his first stage appearance in 1937 at the Empress Theatre, Sutton Coldfield in a Cine Variety Show. He appeared at Theatres and Concert Halls all over the Midlands and area and at the Stage Door Canteen in London, he has also appeared at theatres in Spain and Switzerland.

COURT, Hazel, actress. Born 20 February 1926 in Handsworth, an attractive red head, started her career at the Birmingham Repertory Theatre. Was leading lady in numerous films including "The Mask of Death" with Vincent Price.

DOUGLAS, Alton, comedian, actor, author. Born 22 January 1938 in Small Heath. Educated at St. Benedicts School, Small Heath and at Saltley Grammar School. He has appeared at virtually every major theatre in the U.K. including the London Palladium. T.V. and radio character, BBC Midlands Series of 'Know Your Place'. Served in the Army, 5th Royal Inniskilling Dragoon Guards as a trombonist. Author of "Birmingham at War No. 1 & 2", "Memories of Birmingham", "Coventry at War", "The Black Country at War" and "Memories of Shrewsbury & Coventry", etc. After dinner speaker.

EAVES, Hilary, actress. Born 11 August 1914 in Moseley. Educated at Lowther College, North Wales. Studied for the stage under Kate Rorke and at the Royal Academy of Dramatic Art. Made her first stage appearance at the Hull Repertory Theatre in 1932 in, "The Admirable Crichton". Entered films in 1938, her favourite part being Elizabeth Bennet in, "Pride and Prejudice".

ENGLEMAN, Harry, pianist and band leader. Born 17 January 1912 in Edgbaston. Educated at Tindal Street School, Balsall Heath. Son of Joseph Engleman, composer pianist and violinist. First professional engagement was at the age of 14½ at the Balsall Heath Cinema as relief pianist. At the age of 17 as pianist at the Grand Cinema in his father's orchestra. Renowned broadcaster in Children's Hour in 1934 and Workers Playtime during the last war. Formed his Dance Orchestra in 1936 and his Quintet in 1937. He topped the bill at the London Palladium and performed at numerous venues all over the Midlands and area. Appeared at the Alexandra Palace in London with Jack Wilson, another accomplished pianist in a successful duo. His was the first orchestra to appear on T.V. from the Gosta Green Studio. He served in the RAF during the last war.

FIELD, Sid, comedian. Born 1 April 1904 in Birmingham. Educated at local schools in Sparkbrook area. Made his first stage appearance at the Empire Theatre in Bristol in June 1916 as a member of the 14 Kino Juveniles. He appeared at the Holborn Empire in London the same year. In 1934 he appeared on the stage in Melbourne, Australia. His first film appearance was in the film, "That's My Ticket" made in 1939. He made numerous appearances at all the Birmingham Theatres over the years.

GRANT, Pauline, director and dancer. Born 29 June 1915 in Moseley. Educated at St. Paul's Convent, Edgbaston. Made her first stage appearance at the People's Theatre, St. Pancras, London in December 1937. Became director of Ballet at the Neighbourhood Theatre, Kensington in 1940. Appeared in several films. Was the choreographer to the Shakespeare Memorial Theatre in 1949 and the Glynebourne Opera Festival since 1951. She died in 1986.

HEILBROWN, William, actor. Born 26 June 1879 in Erdington. Made his first stage appearance at the Theatre Royal, Margate on 8 April 1898 as Joshua in "The Arabian Nights" a farcical comedy by Sydney Grundy. In 1901 he appeared at the Surrey Theatre in London as Captain Somers in, "The French Spy", a drama by J.T. Haines. He spent two seasons, period 1929-30 with the Birmingham Repertory Company. In 1941, during the last war, he toured with E.N.S.A. for 6 months. In 1942 he again appeared at the Birmingham Repertory Theatre during the Birmingham Parks Season.

HEYWOOD, Anne, actress (real name Violet Pretty). Born 1931 in Handsworth, educated at Fentham Road Secondary Modern School, Erdington. Was a cinema usherette and beauty queen. Appeared in numerous films including, "90 Degrees in the Shade", "The Chairman" and "The Fox". Resident in Hollywood, U.S.A.

HANCOCK, Tony, comedian. Born 12 May 1924 at 41 Southam Road, Hall Green. A plaque was erected on this house in May 1979 to his memory. He appeared at the Birmingham Hippodrome in 1952 in "Educating Archie". Had his own Radio Series on the BBC entitled "Hancocks Half Hour". He died in Sydney, Australia on the 25 June 1968 aged 44 years.

HUNTLEY, Raymond, actor. Born 23 April 1904 in Birmingham. Educated at King Edward's School in Birmingham. Made his first stage appearance at the Birmingham Repertory Theatre, 1st April 1922, in "A Woman Killed With Kindness", tragedy by Thomas Heywood. Made his first London stage appearance at the Court Theatre on 22 February 1924. Toured the U.S.A. and returned to this country in 1931 and appeared at the Alexandra Theatre, Birmingham playing lead parts. He entered films in 1934 and appeared in numerous pictures.

JACKSON, Sir Barry Vincent, M.A., LL.D., D.Litt., theatre director and dramatic author. Born 6 September 1879 in Birmingham. Was the founder of the Birmingham Repertory Company which commenced operations on 13 February 1913. He was founder of the Pilgrim Players who operated from 16 John Bright Street, Birmingham. He was also the Founder and Director of the Malvern Festivals period 1929-37. He served in the Royal Navy during the 1914-18 War. He was given the Honorary Freedom of the City of Birmingham in 1955. He died on the 3 April 1961.

LAURIER, Jay, actor. Born 31 May 1879 in Birmingham. Made his first stage appearance at the Public Hall in Abertillery in 1896. He was a popular artist in variety and appeared in all the principal music halls in the country and the West End Halls in London. In 1933 he took the part of Buttons in "Cinderella" at the Theatre Royal in Birmingham and in November 1938 took the part of 'Touchstone' in "As You Like It" in the Memorial Theatre in Stratford upon Avon.

LEIGHTON, Margaret, actress. Born on 26 February 1922 in Barnt Green. Educated at the Church of England College in Edgbaston. Made her first stage appearance at the Birmingham Repertory Theatre in September 1938 as Dorothy in, "Laugh With Me". Her first stage appearance in London was on 31 August 1944 as the Troll King's Daughter in, "Peer Gynt". Appeared in several films, her first one was in 1948, "Bonnie Prince Charlie" with David Niven and Jack Hawkins.

MACLEAN, Don, comedian. Born 11 March 1944 in Sparkbrook. Educated at Clifton Road Primary School, St. Philip's Grammar School and Birmingham Theatre School. Made his first stage appearance at the Pier Theatre, Skegness in 'Follies on Parade' in 1964. First T.V. appearance in 'Billy Cotton Band Show' in 1967. Other shows included 'Crackerjack', Black & White Minstrel Show, Mouthtrap, etc. Appeared at the London Palladium 1970 and 75, and in the following theatrical productions, 'Aladdin', 'Cinderella', 'Babes in the Wood', 'Dick Whittington', 'Jack & The Beanstalk', 'Goldilocks', 'Sleeping Beauty', 'Mother Goose' and 'Robinson Crusoe'.

MASCHIWTZ, Eric, O.B.E. Dramatic author. Born in Birmingham 10 June 1901. Educated at Repton School, Gonville and Caius College, Cambridge. He was the Variety Director at the B.B.C. 1933-37. Served in the Intelligence Corps during the last war, rank Lt. Col. He was the Chief Broadcasting Officer in the 21st Army Group in 1945. Has written numerous plays. He was well known under the pseudonym of Holt Marvell.

MATTHISON, Edith Wynne, actress.   Born 23 November 1857 in Birmingham.   Made her first appearance on the stage in Blackpool in December 1896 in, "The School Girl" with Minnie Palmer a musical play by Henry Hamilton and Paul Potter.   She appeared in hundreds of plays in this country and the U.S.A.   She was awarded the gold medal for diction by the American Academy of Arts and Letters in 1927.   She died on the 23 September 1955.

MOONE, Maggie, singer-dancer.   Born 9 July 1953 in Aston.   Her first professional appearance was at the City Varieties Theatre in Leeds.   She was chosen to be a member of the famous Bluebell Girls, and also appeared with the Ballet Bentyber in France.   She has appeared all over the world, endearing herself to international audiences in U.S.A., West Indies, South America, Far East, Africa, and throughout Europe.   T.V. performances included 'Name that Tune', 'The Russ Abbot Show', 'Mike Yarwood Show', 'Morecambe and Wise Show' to name but a few.   Appeared in Derek Salberg's Pantomime at the Princess Theatre, Torquay in the 1969/70 production of "Puss in Boots", and in the pantomime at the Alexandra Theatre in Birmingham in December 1987 "Dick Whittington".

NAPIER, Alan, actor.   Born 7 January 1903 in Harborne.   Educated at Lackwood Haigh and Clifton College.   Studied for the stage at the Royal Academy of Dramatic Arts.   Made his first stage appearance at the Playhouse in Oxford in May 1924 as a policeman in, "Dandy Dick".   His favourite parts were Captain Shotover in "Heartbreak House" and the Marquis of Shayne in "Bitter Sweet".   He has appeared in numerous films.

PEMBERTON, Sir Max, dramatic author and novelist.   Born in Birmingham 19 June 1863.   His first work was "The Diary of a Scoundrel", this was published in 1891.   He was the editor of 'Chums' period 1892-3 and for 10 years 1896-1906 of 'Cassell's Magazine'.   He has written numerous plays and sketches.   Was the founder of the London School of Journalism.

PERRINS, Leslie, actor.   Born in Moseley.   Studied at the Royal Academy of Dramatic Art.   Made his first stage appearance at the Shaftesbury Theatre on 10 January 1922 in "The Rattlesnake".   He has appeared in all the principal theatres in this country and the U.S.A.   Was a prominent member of the BBC Repertory Company.   His film career commenced in 1930 in the film, "The Sleeping Cardinal".

REYNOLDS, Dorothy, actress and author.   Born 26 January 1913 in Birmingham.   Educated at Royal Orphanage, Wolverhampton and the Birmingham University.   Made her first stage appearance in January 1936 when she played Madame Collins in "Payment Deferred" at the Festival Theatre, Cambridge.   She has played in the majority of the major theatres in the U.K.   Her first T.V. appearance was in 1953 when she played the title role in "The Duenna", a comic opera by R.B. Sheridan.   Her books included "Salad Days", "Hooray For Daisy" and "Wildest Dreams".

ROHMER, Sax, dramatic author and novelist.   Born 15 February 1886 in Birmingham.   Educated at King's College.   Author of numerous plays including, "Round the Fifty" in 1922, "The Eye of Siva" in 1923, "Secret Egypt" in 1928.   Has also written numerous lyrics and monologues, including some for George Robey.   His books included "The Mystery of Dr.Fu-Manchu", "The Yellow Claw", "Moon of Madness", etc. to name but a few.

SALBERG, Derek, C.B.E., O.B.E., J.P., theatrical manager and director, author.   Born 30 July 1912 in Birmingham.   Educated at Chigwell House School, Birmingham and Clifton College.   Manager and Director of Alexandra Theatre in Birmingham period 1932-1977.   Member of Warwickshire Cricket Supporters Club since its inception.   Served in the Royal Corps of Signals during the last war, seconded to ENSA when serving in Italy.   Publications, "My Love Affair with a Theatre", "Ring Down the Curtain", "Once upon a Pantomime", "A Mixed Bag" and in 1987 "Much Ado About Cricket".

STIRLING, W. Edward, actor, manager and dramatic author. Born 26 May 1891 in Birmingham. Educated at King Edward VI School in Birmingham. Made his first stage appearance at the Grand Theatre in Wolverhampton on 1 October 1909 as Leonardo in "The Merchant of Venice". His first London stage appearance was at the Scala Theatre on 4 May 1914 as Prince Serpouhousky in "Anna Karenina". He was awarded the honour of Knight of the Order of the Crown from the King of the Belgians in January 1929. He was General Manager of ENSA entertainments in 1944. He published a volume of memoirs in 1945 entitled "Something to Declare".

TYNAN, Kenneth, F.R.S.L., Dramatic critic, author and journalist. Born in Birmingham 2 April 1927. Educated at King Edward's School, Birmingham and at Magdalen College, Oxford. Began his career in 1949 as director of the Lichfield Repertory Company. In May 1951, appeared as the First Player in "Hamlet" with Alec Guiness. He was the drama critic for popular newspapers period 1951-1964. In 1968 he was appointed Literary Manager of the National Theatre in London.

WARD, Dorothy, actress and vocalist. Born 26 April 1890 in Birmingham. Made her first stage appearance at the Alexandra Theatre in Birmingham on 22 December 1905 in "Blue Beard" an extravaganza by H.B. Farnie. She has appeared very successfully as principal boy in over 30 pantomimes in the theatres in the leading provincial cities.

WORDSWORTH, Richard, actor. Born 19 January 1915 in Halesowen Rectory, Worcs. Educated at Loretto and Queen's College, Cambridge. Studied at the Embassy School of Acting. Made his first stage appearance at the Old Vic Theatre in London on 11 October 1938 as Rosencrantz in Hamlet (in modern dress). He played for two seasons at the Memorial Theatre in Stratford upon Avon. He has appeared in numerous films which included "The Man Who Knew Too Much" and "The Quatermass Experiment" he has also made numerous T.V. appearances.

Advertisements from the columns
of pre World War II Birmingham
Newspapers give a good indication
of the number and variety of
theatres, plays and shows available
to the theatregoing public of the day.

Gladys Cooper, D.B.E.

Sir Edward Seymour Hicks

Bransby Williams

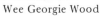

Wee Georgie Wood

Frankie Vaughan

Arthur Askey

Jack Warner

Martin Harvey

Tommy Trinder

Joe Loss

Laurel & Hardy

Elsie and Doris Waters

Gracie Fields, C.B.E.

Winifred Atwell

Tessie O'Shea

Gertie Millar

Dame Flora Robson,
C.B.E., D.B.E.,

The Young Eric Morecambe and Ernie Wise

Ted Ray

Gordon Jackson

Max Miller

ACKNOWLEDGEMENTS

To the editors of the Birmingham Post & Mail, Sunday Mercury, Birmingham Reference Library (Local Studies & Fine Arts Depts.), The Birmingham & Midland Institute, City of Birmingham Development Department, Candid Camera, L. Carter, Alton & Jo Douglas, Jessie Ellerker, S.M. Else, John Hall, J. Hunt, Anne Jennings, Harold Johnson, Gladys Lee, Gina Manly, Dan Pawson, Joyce M. Poole, Florrie Sanders, D. Salberg, J.F. Tozer, Iris Wigley, Maurice White, Albert Williams, Terry Woodcock and my wife Veronica for proof reading the entire book.

COPYRIGHT

from — The End of the Play:

> The play is done; the curtain drops,
> Slow falling to the promter's bell:
> A moment yet the actor stops,
> And looks around, to say farewell.
> It is an irksome word and task:
> And, when he's laughed and said his say,
> He shows, as he removes the mask,
> A face that's anything but gay.

W.M. Thackeray